His Gift

Endorsements

Recently I was asked by a French reporter if I felt myself to be unlucky. I responded with the following: 'No, I am not unlucky. I know God is sovereign. He places us in positions and circumstances to allow his will to be completed in and through our lives.' With this understanding of how our Lord ordains our lives, the question we must ask ourselves is, 'Will I willingly surrender to his will?' In this historical fiction, based on a true story, Molly finds her peace as she yields her talent to the Lord for his use and glory. In the true story upon which *His Gift* is based, Mildred Isle, a gifted musician, finds her fulfillment as a wife, mother, and mentor to many, encouraging all both musically and spiritually.

—**Jim Ryun:** Presidential Medal of Freedom recipient, US Congressman (ret), Multi World Record Holder in the Mile, Half-Mile, 1500m, and 800m, 3xOlympian

Life is a swirling sea of foaming ambiguities, sometimes it's hard to know which end is up or down, and we're often somewhere in the fuzzy in between. In that reality, Joan Benson has crafted *His Gift* to steady your heart and lift your spirit. Her characters are real because she has lived their salty tensions in her soul. Grab a chair, or pillow, and create a space to feel the ups, downs, and fuzzy in between. Visit a slice of not too distant history when faith triumphed over ambiguity and life's meaning could be revealed in a prayer.

—**Rev. Michael Simone**, D.Ministry; author of *Altitude, Your Next Move Changes Everything*; Founding Pastor of Spring Branch Community Church, Virginia Beach, VA; Executive Director of TogoNetwork, mission ministry in Togo, Africa; Adjunct Professor of Religious Studies, Saint Leo University, Norfolk, VA

His Gift is a timely word for those in our culture who are struggling to find hope and faith. The story of Molly's journey will inspire you to use God's gifts, for His glory. As you dedicate those gifts to His service, you will live with a rekindled passion, purpose, and hope.

—**Dr. Will Langford**, lead Pastor of Great Bridge Baptist Church, Chesapeake, VA; Master of Divinity and PhD in Ministry, Baptist Theological Seminary; accomplished author, speaker, and former host of radio program, "Real Conviction"; author of *A Misplaced Trust*.

His Gift captured my heart from the very beginning. Perhaps, it is because I, too, love music and grew up with similar experiences. The love of music, joyful musical mental escape, study in a music conservatory, all balanced against academic demands made "Molly" my kindred spirit. *His Gift* does not ignore the emotional, yet misunderstood, priorities Molly holds. Musical competitions can be unnerving and *His Gift* deeply impacted my soul as I re-tasted the anxiety before Molly's performances. The technically accurate description of the differences between a Steinway and a Baldwin Acrosonic piano waved a blanket of remembrance. Key weight variations do impact the musician's agility, strength, and ability to perform. This book is a must for anyone who played music professionally, is an avid music aficionado, or can appreciate the spiritual journey of a musician.

—**Pat Schneider Wilthew**: Songwriter, composer, producer, author; B.M., M.M.E., Master of Music Education, Old Dominion University, Norfolk, VA; Bachelor of Music Media, Norfolk State University, Norfolk, VA, www.patwilthewmusic.com

Why are so many people intrigued by the character of George Bailey in *It's a Wonderful Life*? He was a talented young man with great dreams who ended up living a very different life than he expected because of the life's unexpected turns. The character of Molly in Joan Benson's book *His Gift* is in many ways a female version of George Bailey. She is a talented young female pianist who wins a student audition for the opportunity to play with the Detroit Symphony. The Great Depression dashed that dream just as it was beginning to blossom. Like George Bailey, Molly must find ways to overcome the grinding disappointment to discover her own wonderful life. Joan Benson has crafted a delightful tale based on her mother's story that is sure to inspire you to pursue your dreams despite all odds.

—**Dr. Craig von Buseck**, author of *I Am Cyrus, Harry S. Truman and the Rebirth of Israel,* and *Nobody Knows: The Harry T. Burleigh Story*

A timely and adventurous story with fun and colorful characters to guide readers through the turbulent times of 1929. Armed with bravery and faith, a young girl faces lost dreams in a changing world—a relevant expression of today's struggles as our youth face the unique challenges of 2020 and beyond.

—**Zanne Marie Dyer**, author of *Dark Motives*, a suspense novel. (Elk Lake Publishing Inc., 2020)

His Gift

Joan C. Benson

Cover and Interior Design: Derinda Babcock

Editor(s): Peggy Ellis, Deb Haggerty

Author Represented By: WordWise Media Services

PUBLISHED BY: Elk Lake Publishing, Inc., 35 Dogwood Drive, Plymouth, MA 02360, 2020

Library Cataloging Data

Names: Benson, Joan C. (Joan C. Benson)

His Gift / Joan C. Benson

244 p. 23cm × 15cm (9in × 6 in.)

Identifiers: ISBN-13: 978-1-64949-030-8 (paperback) | 978-1-64949-031-5 (trade paperback) | 978-1-64949-032-2 (e-book)

Key Words: Young adult, concert piano, 1920s, family, relationships, career goals, Great Depression

LCCN: 2020942707 Fiction

Dedication

With love to my mother, Mildred M. Isle, an enduring and creative woman who fearlessly spoke her mind and firmly embraced her faith in Jesus Christ. You rooted me in love, gave me confidence to achieve, and pointed the way to Christ as my ultimate source of all good. We miss you, but we rest in the knowledge of a wonderful heavenly reunion.

Table of Contents

Preface

In the fall of 2006, I had the privilege of visiting Royal Oak and Detroit, Michigan. Royal Oak was a beautiful, well-kept little suburb, with obvious care and upkeep of the bungalow style homes so common in the twentieth century Midwest. My husband and I visited the beautiful Detroit Symphony Hall and came to appreciate its outstanding architecture. I dug deeply into microfiche records at the Detroit Public Library to help me accurately portray the era.

With the caring assistance of a Royal Oak resident and local historian, Ms. Lois Lance, I researched much of the information to add authenticity to the story. Ms. Lance was a storehouse of historical details. During our interview, she confirmed that Royal Oak High School was new and beautiful in 1929, transportation to Detroit was reasonable and safe, and dating was often a group social situation, with singing and piano accompaniment a common element. Many of her details have embellished the plot of His Gift.

In October 1929, according to family history, my mother, Mildred White Isle, won the Student Audition to play the Rachmaninoff Concerto with the Detroit Symphony. She and her parents lived in the bedroom community of Royal Oak, and she studied at their Conservatory of Music, with early release time from high school for her piano study, as the main character Molly did.

My mother, portrayed by Molly, had aspired to become a concert pianist, but the Great Depression denied her that possibility. However, she continued sharing her gift for music as she became a wife and mother. She taught piano at MacMurray College in Jacksonville, Illinois, as a young mother, and later became a longstanding member of the Accredited Music Teachers Association in Lawrence, Kansas. Mildred continued teaching piano into her final year of life, age eighty-two.

My mother's lost dream of concertizing was impactful, but with faith in Christ, she found her way forward to a fulfilling life. Mildred was a positive force as she lived her faith and shared her gift of music with so many. Her son later became a professional musician, carrying her legacy into the next generation.

Acknowledgments

I have many people to thank who made this dream possible. I am thankful I met David Fessenden, my agent with Wordwise Media, who chose to represent me as a first-time author though my chances looked slim. Thank you, David, for your encouragement along the way and for loving the story. I owe a debt of thanks to Deb Ogle Haggerty, Publisher and Editor in Chief; Peggy Ellis, my thoughtful and meticulous editor; and everyone at Elk Lake Publishing for believing in my story.

The writing of His Gift began many years ago after my mother passed away, and I reflected on her life. However, the rudimentary manuscript kept ending up in a drawer, sometimes for months and sometimes for years, as more pressing matters took precedence in my life. After writing about half, I realized the book was not simply a moral story for young adults, my original goal, but contained a spiritual conflict. I thank God for the inspiration to write the final chapters of the book. I believe he stirred the ideas for the resolution of this real-life conflict, when on my own, I had no idea what to do.

I thank my husband, Jan, for accompanying me on a long road trip to Michigan, as I researched the setting in Royal Oak and Detroit. I returned armed with details necessary to tell the story with historical accuracy.

I thank Craig von Buseck, author, speaker, teacher, and mentor, for his encouragement and wise advice in our Christian Writers' Group. He helped me realize, though one can revise forever, there comes a time to conclude, knowing one's next book will be even better.

I thank my friend and loyal supporter, Jim Ryun, who shared his parallel journey in athletics (three-time Olympian runner) with my mother's passion and talent in music. Thank you, Jim and Anne, for sharing your testimony of the sovereignty of God working in your lives.

I thank all my loyal readers and faithful followers who gave me their insights and wise comments to help create the best manuscript possible: Elaine Johnson, Diana Randall, Laura Blank, Marjorie Wingert, Pat Wilthew, Candance Moore, my brother, Robert Isle, my patient husband, Jan Benson, and many others who encouraged me from the onset of my writing.

Chapter 1—Ready or Not

The audition, the Audition, the AUDITION … October 12, 1929, was only two days away, but it had been penned in my diary for two years. With almost a thousand hours of practice behind me, I knew my destiny hung in the balance.

The bell rang. I scooped up my things and made a beeline to the door. The staff at the Music Conservatory frowned upon tardiness. Could I prove I was ready for Saturday?

"Molly Martin—a word, please." Mr. Hill stepped into my path, blocking my exit from class. I glanced at the clock, but I didn't need a reminder. I only had fifteen minutes.

"I have to run, Mr. Hill. Remember my permission for early-release on Mondays and Thursdays?"

Draping the lab coat over his arm, Mr. Hill looked aloof, yet stern. He towered above me with his tall, skinny frame. He ignored the students edging around us to get on to their classes. Some students called Mr. Hill 'the teacher with no soul.' I would add he had no heart if he made me late for my pre-audition at the Music Conservatory.

"I'm confused, Miss Martin. Why are you taking this chemistry class?" he said, as if to pique my defense.

Good question. Did he think I would admit my parents insisted? I held my tongue. My parents drilled respect into me from childhood.

The fleeing students glanced with curiosity as they

brushed by. Talking. Laughing. Being normal. My instinct was to escape this confrontation, but I stood rooted to my spot.

"I believe you're a smart girl," he said. The smell of stale coffee wafted in the air as he waved his hand in exasperation.

Apparently, I was not smart enough to escape his little lecture.

"Thank you, sir," I replied, with dramatic pretense.

"You can do so much better. You know that you need a passing grade to be accepted by a worthy college."

So they say. "With all due respect, sir, my goal is to win the competition with the Detroit Symphony Orchestra." Everyone knew that. Even the principal. "College is not in my sights after graduation," I stated with conviction. "At least not right away."

I stepped forward. Surely, we were finished.

Mr. Hill held up one hand to stop me. "And, if you don't win this audition, Molly?"

The Detroit Symphony Orchestra held one student competition each year. Only one. My hopes hung on this audition. As a senior, I needed to win. This time. I knew many girls hoped to marry when they graduated. A few would go to college. Not me. Not now.

"You're way behind in this class, Molly."

Wiggling his fingers in the air as if playing an imaginary piano, his head shook and his eyes crinkled shut. "Your entire life is about—this."

"I am serious about this, sir. What is wrong with concentrating on one's strengths?"

"You are shortsighted, Miss Molly. Out of balance." He tossed his coat a few feet behind us, barely landing it on the lectern.

"Excuse me," someone whispered. By now students

from the next class were squeezing in.

"With respect, I do have goals and priorities, Mr. Hill."

"Do you even take time for friends, Molly?"

"Thank you for your wise advice, Mr. Hill."

By then, my words were dripping with sarcasm. His disapproving black eyes glared back, and for an instant, his bushy eyebrows raised.

Mama and Father would be furious if they had heard me speak to a teacher in this manner. But what was he thinking to insult me like that? No friends? What did he know about my life? My words spilled out before I could snatch them back.

With a sigh, Mr. Hill spewed out his final chiding remark. "You may be an expert with the keys of the piano." He wiggled his fingers in a mocking gesture. "But I fear you know nothing about the keys to life. You'd better find a tutor before the next grading period."

Arguing at this point would prolong my agony. I kept my mouth closed. I nodded, giving a polite, but phony, smile.

"Miss Martin, do you understand me?"

"Yes, sir," I replied, glancing at the clock again. In silence, I made clear I was finished. My fifteen minutes of travel time was now down to ten. Besides, the seats were filling up with his next class. He had no choice. He had to release me from captivity.

"All right, Miss Molly. Don't force my hand. If you fail another test, the principal has agreed your privilege for early release must end. I'll spell it out for you. No more piano lessons on school time, no matter how gifted you are." This time he looked at me with a sorrowful expression. Or maybe it was pity. He stepped back and waved his arm toward the doorway.

Was he sad because he wanted me to see the error of my ways and embrace his fervent zeal for chemistry? This self-appointed resident scientist presumed nothing in the world was more important than chemistry. Yet he lectured me on balance? "The keys of life," I should say. Maybe he had breathed in too many chemicals hanging over Bunsen burners. I couldn't worry with his attitude right then. Mr. Clancy had precious few extended timeslots for advanced students, so I had to protect my chance to train with such an experienced professional.

I fled for my locker, grabbed my music, and pushed through the massive double doors of Royal Oak High. Freedom. Ahhh—delightful. Brisk fall breezes whipped at my open wool jacket. I flung my scarf around my neck as an added layer while I buttoned up.

No more thoughts about school. The tension with Mr. Hill must not ruin my lesson. The concerto's familiar melody began playing in my mind, pushing my steps ever faster to its pulsing rhythm. As the upcoming competition demanded my attention, I wondered if this is how Olympic athletes felt. Excited? Tense? A little bit anxious?

If I won, I would perform with the Detroit Symphony at their annual student performance concert in January. As a young classical pianist, this concert would be my best hope for recognition.

Rachmaninoff's Concerto #2 possessed me, but in a good way, not like Mr. Hill described. If I closed my eyes, I could imagine the bold and beautiful sounds of the concerto with the orchestra accompanying me. Mama had taken me to the symphony last winter when Rachmaninoff played his own masterpiece. I fell in love. In that moment. I knew that someday I had to perform this magnificent composition.

I wanted to show Mr. Clancy I was ready. This would be like a pre-audition audition. I needed to prove I could do this for myself even more than for dear Mr. Clancy. I stretched my fingers open and closed in preparation for the keyboard gymnastics and quickened my gait to more of a controlled dash.

In the distance, I could see the Music Conservatory. The building overshadowed the bungalow-type homes nestled around it. Teaching rooms were in the front of the house and living quarters for the teachers in the back. The studio seemed warm and bright, even during our long, cold winters. I took the front steps by twos, and could hear Mr. Clancy playing while he waited. A familiar Mozart Sonata intermingled with another student's repetitive finger exercises from an adjacent studio.

"Mr. Clancy?" I called as I entered the front hall. I closed the front door firmly, so the chilly air would not seep in. "It's Molly."

"Yes, yes, my dear, but you are late. Time is wasting. Come right on over to the piano." Mr. Clancy, already seated at his prized Steinway grand, ran his leathery, wrinkled fingers up and down the keys with ease as if to encourage me to begin.

His sharp, distinctive nose swept in the direction of the baby-sized grand piano as my signal to sit down. The small studio was crammed with two grand pianos filling most every inch, but for me, the place brought great joy. I slipped between the gleaming instruments to find my place. Busts of the masters, Beethoven, Mozart, and Rachmaninoff, watched me with their marble gazes. To prepare my hands for the challenge, I ran through some warm-up exercises. Then Mr. Clancy stood, nodding for me to begin. I lifted my hands over the keys and whispered, "Please God." He knew.

I pressed into the dramatic opening chords, Rachmaninoff's invitation to enter his composition. Nothing less than perfection was necessary to perform the many intricate runs to follow. Each note had to sing, producing the unique resonating tones of a Steinway grand piano. In a matter of seconds, my left hand stumbled on a lengthy run. I stopped and glanced nervously at Mr. Clancy.

"I am so sorry," I blurted. "I had a problem at school, which also caused me to be late."

Mr. Clancy calmly held up his hand. "Breathe deeply, and begin again."

It sounded simple, yet …

Okay. I refuse to let anything derail me, even for one moment. Mr. Clancy stood waiting. Tilting his chin upward, he closed his eyes. Did he believe I was capable of winning? Did he worry that I might embarrass him?

I began playing the deep, resonating chords again. This time, as the sounds swelled to a crescendo, my confidence rose. At last, my hands took charge in an inexplicable way as a consequence of mastery. My fingers nearly operated without my conscious mind controlling their movement.

From the corner of my eye, I saw Mr. Clancy settle back at his piano. Like the master he was, he knew where to join in, accompanying me with the orchestra melody. Before long, the passion of Rachmaninoff's creation spilled into every inch of the room from floor to ceiling. From keyboard to keyboard, the moving musical theme tossed back and forth. The thrill of creating such beauty with a full symphony orchestra captured my imagination even as I played in this tiny studio.

Leaning into the keyboard, I formed the spirited chords with precision, thundering into the final stretch of the first movement as Rachmaninoff had done. Then silence. Utter silence. The first third of this mighty work was gloriously finished in barely over thirty minutes. Though there was not time enough to play all three sections, my need was to demonstrate preparedness. Resting my hands on the keys for a moment, I relaxed and set them in my lap with a quiet sigh. Anxious for his approval, I stole a fleeting look at Mr. Clancy. He rose with the awkward stiffness characteristic of many his age. His mouth gaped open in gleeful delight. My fond old mentor lifted his arms heavenward and began clapping. At first lightly, and then with unrestrained abandon.

"Bravo, Molly! Bravo! Outstanding. What an accomplishment."

"Thank you," I said struggling for composure. "If only I can play so well on Saturday."

My mind and heart were shouting and dancing, though I restrained myself as the maturing young adult I wanted to be. But I did get up and give Mr. Clancy an enthusiastic thank you hug. Before I left, Mr. Clancy gave me some practice tips before the audition. He warned against only practicing the piece, but instructed me to play a variety of music to maintain my finger agility. Oh, how I wished I had the artistic and physical skill of Rachmaninoff himself. Writing this concerto for his own oversized hands, Rachmaninoff was capable of reaching across large spans of keys. His music presented so many physical challenges for pianists, especially a girl with a smaller frame like me.

"I don't know how to thank you enough. You've been so helpful. Are you going to make it to Detroit for the audition?" I asked.

"I'd love to be there Saturday, but my old arthritic back won't allow it. Believe me. I know auditions. There will be lots of hours of waiting around that is characteristic of all auditions." He raised one of his white bushy eyebrows, and leaned in closer to me.

"I'll come hear you play with the symphony after you win the contest," he whispered as if telling a secret.

"Do you believe I could possibly win?"

He smiled his gentle kind of smile accompanied by an assenting tilt of his head. With the polite bow of a gentleman, Mr. Clancy then escorted me to the door with a performer's send off. "Believe in yourself. And, don't stop breathing," he said chuckling.

Though Mr. Clancy was a gifted professional musician, he was so much more to me—a friend, a grandfather-type, an encourager, and a sweet old man. With a wave and smile, I skipped down the front steps of the Conservatory, my feet floating like feathers. I knew I had Mr. Clancy's affirmation so all I had to do was believe and breathe, and I might add, pray. I'd done my homework on this one.

The fall sun had already dipped below the horizon when I began the walk home. The glowing lights and savory smells of burning fireplaces in the homes along the way invited my curiosity. I wondered what real life dramas would take place inside those bungalows in the coming days.

I knew I had my own melodrama to work out. Father and Mama were usually supportive of my music, but I also knew their concern for my future. Everyone acknowledged my lack of interest in academics. Of course, even I would be embarrassed if I didn't graduate. But, study? Right now? Oh, gee—not one of my priorities. I would catch up in chemistry somehow enough to pass, at least. Most of all, I would become a concert pianist. Maybe I would cross over on a great ship to London or Paris, or perhaps I would perform in Vienna, Austria, like many great musicians.

Spotting our porch light a few doors down, I slowed

my steps. An uneasiness jolted me back to my present-day realities and the confrontation with Mr. Hill, but there seemed to be something more. Mama always talked about her woman's intuition as she seemed to have a double dose of it. Maybe I had it too. Things didn't look right as I approached our house. Father was home.

It wasn't time for him to be back from work, yet I saw the old 1925 Packard parked in the drive. I circled around to the back porch, and saw Mama through the kitchen window. Wait. She was crying. Not onion-tears. Real tears. I could hear the thumping of my anxious heart.

As I crept up the back steps, they let out a warning creak. Mama glanced up as I cracked open the door. She looked back at the skillet where she had been stirring the hash. Mama swiped at her eyes with the apron like she always did when she chopped onions.

"Mama, what in the world?

Chapter 2—Secret Plans

"Please go ahead and wash up, Molly," Mama said, trying to sound nonchalant. "It's almost five-thirty, and your father needs his supper on time."

I had only seen Mama in tears one other time in all of my almost eighteen years. That had been the awful week after my grandma passed away. Now, as she turned toward me, I could see her puffy eyes betraying her gentle smile. Something wasn't right. Should I go along with her pretense or dig for the truth? Did I want to know? Mama looked beautiful, as always, but she didn't realize the shadow of sorrow I saw on her face. I pasted a little fake joy over my own sense of worry to test the waters.

"Mmmmm. Supper smells good, Mama," I said with as much cheer as my heart could muster.

"Thank you, Molly."

Then, hesitating, I dared. "May I ask why you seem upset? Is something wrong with Father?"

"We're fine, Molly. Would you please call him for supper? Everything is about ready to dish up."

I tried imagining what was wrong as I approached the living room. Father sat in his easy chair, head back, eyes closed, spectacles dangling from one hand.

I placed my hand on his shoulder gently. I didn't want to alarm him. "Father?"

"Oh—uh—hmm," he said, startled from his own inner thoughts.

"Mama says supper is almost ready."

"I'll be right there," he said, clearing his throat from his dozing state. He lurched forward from his chair while smoothing his hair back into place. He seemed embarrassed to have me find him in his own world of sleep, or maybe he was sorting through everything happening.

I returned to the kitchen, usually a private place for Mama and me. Just us alone. Tonight, I didn't even try talking to her, but went to work on my chores. I pulled out our standard red-checked oil cloth from its drawer and covered our dining room table. Next, came Mama's painstakingly hand-embroidered napkins upon which I placed the flatware. Hearing Father's feet shuffling in our direction, Mama spoke up.

"Your favorite corned beef hash and green beans, Hank. They should cheer you."

Father always looked forward to a hot supper when he came home from work, and Mama happily obliged him.

"Good evening, again, Father," I called out as he approached.

He didn't reply, but headed into the kitchen to wash his hands, acknowledging me with a faint smile. I arranged a generous serving of green beans around a mound of the corned beef hash. Mama carried in a basket of piping hot biscuits. We took our usual places around the old oak table outfitted for the occasion. Thankfully some things were as consistent as clockwork.

"Molly, please bless the food," Father said, extending his hands to join with ours.

"Of course," I answered, bowing my head.

"Dear Father in Heaven, thank you for the bounty you have given us and for the delicious food you've provided. I pray we might serve you well. Amen."

Father immediately started talking. He seemed rattled by something going on with the stock market. As far as I knew, my parents didn't invest in stocks like rich people did, so it didn't seem too much of a threat to us. Why was he disturbed about this?

While they talked, my mind drifted back to the details of my fickle day. Down. And then up. Now this mysterious veil over all that should have been routine at home.

"Molly, how is everything at school?" Father asked, invading my thoughts.

Surprised by the sudden attention, I nearly gagged on the bite of hash I had put in my mouth. Fortunately, while I chewed, I could consider my answer. Timing is everything.

"Fine, Father. I'm fine," I said, trying to muster confidence. "I went to the Conservatory today for my final lesson. Mr. Clancy and I played the concerto together—better than I've ever played it before."

I had avoided the school subject rather deftly, I thought. I felt blood rush to my head and wondered if anyone noticed my blush. Mama seemed to stare at me. She knew me better than anyone else in the world. I needed to resolve my problem before Mr. Hill squelched my early release or contacted my parents.

"That is wonderful, Molly," Father answered, glancing over at Mama.

"Is it this Saturday that you two are going into Detroit?" he asked, directing his question to Mama.

"Yes, dear," she said, with a gentle smile.

"Let's hope the symphony is still funded after these days of dropping prices on the stock market," he said, barely audible. "I don't know what is going on ..."

"Oh, Hank, I'm sure things will work out. Let's don't bring up discouraging thoughts because today was difficult,"

Mama piped in. "Things always get better, don't they?"

"We have to understand what is happening and prepare for the worst," Father said raising his volume a bit.

Father had my attention. My head popped up as I tuned out my own thoughts about Saturday.

"Why are you saying the stock market could impact the symphony, Father?"

"Well, the symphony needs their patrons to have money to buy tickets, Molly. They need the money to pay the musicians' salaries. If the economy continues to choke up like this, then everyone loses."

Father continued to eat with that stoic expression parents get when they don't want to talk to you.

"Tasty hash, Ruth."

"May I please be excused?" I asked as soon as it seemed acceptably polite to do so. I didn't want to listen to Father's depressing dialogue when I had the audition and my school problem to wrestle with.

"Of course, Molly," Mama said, glancing at Father for his approval. Mama wouldn't expect me to help in the kitchen tonight with the audition only two days away. She also wouldn't be suspicious of my need to be excused early.

Of course, I would practice. However, I also needed to talk to my best friend, Winifred, about chemistry class. Winnie, as we called her, was not only my trusted friend, she was much more inclined to do well in school. We had known each other from early childhood, and Winnie was like the sister I never had. We shared our most intimate thoughts, laughed like hyenas at funny things, and stood behind each other with fierce loyalty through good times and bad.

With Mama and Father still talking, they wouldn't overhear me because the phone was down the hall toward our bedrooms. A cute little arched cubby had been built flush into the wall, a perfect fit for the telephone. Mama had found a very small bench to tuck in there, but often I sat on the floor. Sadly, when I picked up the phone, all I heard were chattering voices. Party lines. When you want to talk and can't, it is not a party. Badly named, I'd say. It seemed that whenever I wanted to make a call, someone else was on the phone. With five families on the same line, it was nearly impossible to connect when I needed to.

I walked to my baby grand looming over the other furnishings in the living room. In a small house like ours, the piano dwarfed everything else, and its tones reverberated from wall to wall, room to room. Mama would wonder if I didn't begin practicing right away.

I began with some finger drills on the keys just as Mr. Clancy suggested. I had to do these hand-strengthening exercises every day, so my mind wandered, relying on memory to propel my fingers forward. Dear Jack popped into my mind while I performed the drills. I met him in study hall last year, and he used to help me out with geometry. I never really understood the formulas, but he was so adorable. I could tell he liked me because he always looked for me in the halls and would wave me down. After some months, we began meeting after school almost daily.

On this important day, we missed our usual locker time because I left school early. Jack often waited for me so we could walk part way home together. He was such a cute and positive guy, always ready with a smile and kind word. Nice, but I had no time for boys.

I caught myself daydreaming, devouring precious time. Time to get serious about schoolwork and contact Winnie. Before I realized, an hour had evaporated, and I hadn't even tried calling Winnie back. By that time, Mama and Father were situated in the easy chairs, reading the newspaper.

I slipped out to try the phone again, hopefully unnoticed. I did not want my parents to hear our private conversation. I reached for the bell-shaped receiver hanging on its hook stand. Our old phone had been replaced in the summer with an updated version. Now I could dial the numbers instead of waiting for the operator to call. The phone was ringing through. Relief.

"Hel-lo."

"Winnie?"

"Oh, Molly, great to hear from you. How did your pre-audition go this afternoon?"

"It went very well. Thank you for asking. But that's not why I'm calling. I have a huge favor to ask. Can we meet early tomorrow morning?"

"Was Mr. Hill acting up again? What's so awful that you can't tell me now?"

"Winnie, shhh! I really need to see you in person. We're still on a p-a-r-t-y-l-i-n-e," I said, reminding her of our lack of privacy. "And besides, I must do some homework before I go to bed."

"Of course. I'll meet you in the morning," Winnie said. "I'll be praying for you."

"Thanks. See you at your locker before class."

I went to my bedroom feeling a bit more hopeful than when I left school. Winnie was a good student, and if anyone could help, she could. I still had a history chapter to read before bedtime, but I could handle that.

After reading the first few pages, I realized I didn't retain a blessed thing. Something about Egyptian pharaohs, but I couldn't tell you why they were important. Sigh. I started at the beginning again in hopes of capturing more of it the second time. Before I knew it, my head was down, my eyes closed. A familiar melody began running through my brain. Names of famous classical composers marched in and out: "Mozart, Beethoven, Bach, Tchaikovsky, Rachmaninoff … I needed to sleep. Then, maybe, the pharaohs would find their important places in civilization as well as my brain.

Visualizing the stage in Detroit's Orchestra Hall, that magnificent building where the greatest of musicians had performed, I imagined myself thundering through the final notes of the concerto. I even imagined Jack in the audience, waiting with a bouquet of roses. How much fun that would be. But then an unpleasant image flashed upon the tablet of my mind. A grim Mr. Hill holding up a periodic table of chemical elements—no smile, and no applause for my best musical efforts. Horror of horrors. Poof. My daydream vanished.

Shutting my history book with disgust, I knew I hadn't accomplished a thing. I crawled under my covers and prayed.

Thank you, God, for giving me blessings for this day, despite the worries. Thank you for Mr. Clancy's kindness, and for music, which thrills my soul. Thank you for the gift of Sergei Rachmaninoff and what you inspired him to create. Amen.

I knew what I had to do. I had to keep concentrating. Not on Mr. Hill. Not on homework. Not on the stock market, whatever all the hullabaloo was about. I threw back the covers and pulled my diary out of the drawer. I stared at the entry I made two years ago on the very first page. "My life will begin or end on October 12, 1929." Those thoughts were written so long ago, but now here I was, just days away. I had to keep my attention fixed on my goal.

I slipped out of my room and tiptoed down the darkened hallway to the bathroom for a final drink. I could see the living room light, so Father was still up. That was unusual. Mama and Father's bedroom door was closed, but a narrow beam of light peeked out from under it. I heard Mama's voice and leaned closer to the door. Was it wrong to listen? Probably. Well, definitely. I had been taught better. But maybe I could discover what had been troubling her. Leaning in, I heard Mama's voice praying softly.

"Sweet Jesus. You know how hard she's worked for this. Please help her accomplish her dreams."

It was clear she was praying for me. I felt warm inside, like Mama had given me a real hug.

"She needs this, Lord. And she is so close."

I placed my ear snug against the wood door and hoped Father wouldn't suddenly appear.

"Yet why do I feel something is wrong?" Mama went on.

Wait. What was she saying? What could be wrong? I scooted to my bedroom before I compounded my problems by getting caught. My settled confidence vanished. Maybe this was my consequence for eavesdropping.

"You have nothing to worry about, Molly. You have nothing to worry about." I whispered to myself. Hearing those words spoken helped me believe them, yet the warm, positive feeling I had only moments earlier had melted into the darkness.

Chapter 3—Mama

A heavy melancholy wrapped around me like a blanket when I awakened in the morning. Things were not right. Of course, I still had no insight. Gathering myself out from the warmth of my bedcovers, I convinced myself I would not worry. I needed to get things done.

"Molly? Hurry now. It's time for breakfast," Mama called from the kitchen.

"Coming."

My grandma used to say Mama saw the world through rose-colored glasses. For years, I didn't understand what she meant. I could see Mama didn't wear eyeglasses, but as I matured, I understood how right Grandma was. Mama saw beauty in everything. Even her rosy glasses weren't enough to tint her perspective now, or she wouldn't have been praying with such fervor last night. Oh, how I needed her to have confidence things would be fine, or even better, wonderful. If Mama had no hope, would I have enough on my own?

I followed the delicious scents wafting down the hallway, a comfort in itself. The dining room was quiet because Father left for work early, but Mama didn't explain why.

"Thank you," I said, as I sat down to a breakfast of cinnamon toast and oatmeal.

In solitude, I ate while she puttered with clean up. Mama's soft voice halted my ponderings.

"Molly, dear, would you enjoy taking the day off?" Mama asked with a gleam in her eyes. "I took Father to work early, so we have the car. What would you think of getting a new finger wave for your hair before your big day tomorrow? We can get your new hairdo, eat lunch at the café, and spend some time together."

From her tone of voice, it sounded like last night's drama was behind us. This was a puzzling turnabout from the sadness I had felt. I peered up from my breakfast, smiling, desperate to read Mama's face for motive. But my plans. I had to meet with Winnie. The next chemistry quiz was on Wednesday and time was crucial. Before I could consider beginning as a concert artist, I knew Mama and Father would demand I graduate.

"Mama, that sounds like fun. I would love to try the finger wave style, which would dress up my boring straight hair," I said, still wondering if we were playing charades. "Do you think you could get an appointment for me after school instead? Big test on Wednesday."

I must have sounded convincing because she didn't question my uncommon concern about school.

"I'll check with Jayne and see if she has time for you later this afternoon, sweetheart. I understand if you want to keep yourself occupied at school today. You must have a few jitters.

I would normally snatch any opportunity to stay home to read, practice, or do things with Mama. She never had qualms about taking me out of school for an occasional day together. I loved that she valued our time more than a day of school. One time, we went to lunch at the Hudson Hotel dining room in Detroit. I got one of those new Charleston-style bobs that day. The haircut, named for the dance, was a little longer, fluffier 'do that bounced when we kicked and hitched. Cute. The finger wave was tight against the head, and a little dressier looking, I thought.

I would have to say Mama was one of my best "friends." Not a girlfriend like Winnie, with whom I shared everything in confidence, but she was a fun mother. Despite her placid life, she loved having a good time. Anytime friends gathered, Mama became the life of the party with her music. She would plunk out whatever Tin Pan Alley tunes people wanted her to play on the piano. That's a different kind of talent from mine. She couldn't read one line of notes, let alone play Rachmaninoff, but she could hear a song once and recreate the chords and melody.

Good grief. After all our scheming, I was almost late for school. Gathering my books from the dining room table, I pleaded, "Mama, could you please, please drive me to school this morning since you have the car?"

She looked at the clock and chuckled. "Look, our carriage is waiting, Molly, my beautiful Cinderella."

Restless as a kitten, I fidgeted on the car ride, praying I would still see Winnie before classes.

"Molly, why are you so anxious today? You've never been so concerned about school in the past."

"Oh, nothing really. I just need to check on something before my first class. Thanks for helping out."

It seemed like Mama was driving slower than ever, making cautious stops at every intersection. Would we ever get there? Mama must have taken her Cinderella carriage joke to heart. The first bell rang as I scurried down to our usual meeting place. I could see Winnie from the back, walking on toward her first class.

"Winnie, wait!" I cried, picking up my pace while trying not to make a spectacle of myself.

"Molly, I was worried about you," she said, turning around in surprise.

"It's okay, Winnie. Here's a short SOS note. We can talk

at lunch."

Squishing a small folded paper into Winnie's palm, I told her to read it whenever she could. We both hurried away, realizing we'd no doubt be tardy. Mr. Hill had promised to call my parents if I didn't improve, but then again, if I won the audition on Saturday, would they care? I would hold onto that happy thought.

My morning classes were not thrilling. English, Latin, and history. In history, Mr. Patterson asked anyone who had not read the chapter to leave for study hall. Another girl and I raised our hands.

I did not retain what I'd read the night before anyway. It's a wonder the whole class didn't raise their hands because in all honesty, Mr. Patterson was about the most boring teacher ever. He often stared out the window and spoke in a monotone. How dull. Maybe he was apathetic about history too. What an odd thought. At least he was always kind, nothing like Mr. Bunsen Burner.

When the lunch bell rang, I flew out of class.

"Excuse me. Excuse me," I said, jostling around a slower pack of socializing students. Time was short.

"There you are," I called out to Winnie, waving from a distance. She waited for me to catch up.

"Molly, let's walk over to Sanders Soda Fountain. We can get a hot chocolate with our sandwiches."

"Wonderful. They have the best of the best hot chocolates."

Most everybody liked to sit on the barstools, so for privacy, we chose a booth against the wall.

"So," Winnie began. "Are you failing?"

Winnie stared me straight in the eyes. Before I could answer her blunt question, the waitress came.

"What would you girls like today?"

"Two hot chocolates, please," I answered.

"No lunches today?"

"No, thank you," we chimed in unison.

The waitress turned to leave, and Winnie shifted her piercing gaze back at me. She was always such a Goodie Two-Shoes, she would never ever get behind in her school work.

She drilled me again. "Back to your problem, Molly," she redirected. "Did Mr. Hill say you are failing?" She didn't sound angry, but it was clear she meant business.

"No, but it may to come to that. He stopped me as I was on my way to the Conservatory. Mr. Hill lectured me, right in front of all the students. I tried to explain. His only answer was to tell me I'd better find a tutor. Winnie, you know how strict the policies are at the Conservatory. It's a privilege to study there, and being late is not acceptable."

"Molly. the audition will be over Saturday, but you still have to finish high school."

"Well, I was hoping you could tutor me. You understand chemistry. I want to put high school behind me, and this is a way."

"I can try to help, but how are you going to catch up now? I cannot imagine teaching you everything in three days. Our mid-terms are next week."

"I don't know. I don't know. I can only hope it will work," I said softly, breathing a silent prayer.

The waitress arrived with our piping hot chocolates dotted with a spoonful of whipping cream. Oh yum. What a delicious distraction. Hoping nobody would notice, we slipped our bologna sandwiches out of our purses and nibbled as discreetly as possible.

Somehow, I felt more confident as we headed back to school that afternoon. Winnie gave me a quick hug accompanied by her signature wink of encouragement.

"You'll impress the judges tomorrow. I know you will."

"Please pray for me. Thanks, Winnie."

When I went to chemistry that day, Mr. Hill was stern, but polite. Mama always told me to pray for my enemies. Was Mr. Hill my enemy? I suppose not. Maybe he didn't understand the stakes. Then again, he probably wouldn't care. My world was not his world.

My life seemed to be such a messy business, tortuous, with many loose ends and unconnected dots. I promised myself I would begin concentrating on school after the audition. And with that extra push, I would show Mr. Hill a thing or two on Wednesday.

I couldn't stay back to see Jack after school though, and I had missed him at lunch. Oh, well. Jack and I were only friends, so not a big upset. But, just in case, a note would have to do.

> Dear Jack, I need to rush out today. Hope you are fine. I have a hair appointment after school today. Fondly, Molly.

I scribbled a smiling face on the bottom of my roughly drafted note. No hearts though. Heavens. That would be way too forward.

I slipped the paper into the air slots of Jack's locker,where I knew he'd find it. That's how he always left notes for me.

"Mama, I'm home. Were you able to get my hair appointment?" I called.

"Yes, Molly," Mama answered.

I peered into the living room where Mama sat, legs curled up in the easy chair. She was reading yet another novel. Mama always had her nose in a book when she wasn't keeping up with housework and gardening.

"We can go over together, if you'd like. Your appointment is at three o'clock," she added.

We chatted about our day as we walked the four blocks to Miss Mansard's Beauty Shop. The sun was shining, but the air was crisply cool. Inside the shop, the ladies were buzzing with the news of the day.

"What do you think about the stock market fall, Ruth?" Jayne asked. With care, she pressed each wave of my hair into place with her fingers before combing out the next strand. A little homemade gel secured each wave.

"Well, Hank did tell me about a downturn in the prices, Jayne. I wouldn't worry too much. You know how the business world is. Up and down, up and down."

Everyone seemed to nod in silent assent. The room grew still as such weighty news was digested. Miss Mansard continued transforming my straight hair in a methodical rhythm.

Suddenly Mrs. Burr, who was getting a haircut, piped up. We always referred to her as Mrs. Nosey since she knew everybody's business. Heads usually turned when she spoke.

"Well, I heard yesterday the Heiss family over on Mohawk Street have already hit some hard times."

Miss Mansard stared at her with that silencing kind of look parents give. "Now, now, Doris, we really shouldn't be passing around other people's business. We might get the facts mixed up. That wouldn't be good for anyone, would it?"

Mrs. Nosey's cheeks flushed pink but didn't stop her from sharing her latest gossip.

"I thought maybe we should ask if there is anything we could do. If you lost your job and home, wouldn't you want someone to bring you a meal or at least listen to your problems?"

Silence fell again. Mama broke the awkward moment with her Pollyanna goodness.

"Maybe we should all be praying for each other, for the President, and for our country. I simply refuse to believe President Hoover will let things get too far out of hand," Mama said.

Her words hung in the air, suspended, for us to absorb. Was she right? I felt an urgency to finish and leave. Mrs. Nosey was such a bother. Honestly. She worked for the telephone company and was the worst busybody in town. Mrs. Mansard turned everyone's attention back to my life for a positive sendoff.

"We wish you well tomorrow, Molly, as you compete for the Student Audition. I can only imagine the excitement you feel. There now," she said, patting the last wave into place. "You will look precious as you play."

The beauty shop ladies sent us off with good wishes for my important day, and Mama and I began a casual stroll back to the house. I felt peaceful again, just Mama and me, talking about ordinary life. Boys, hairstyles, clothes, and such. We left behind the negative thoughts. No major cares in those quiet moments.

Royal Oak was named for its graceful old oak trees lining its streets. Their leaves, dressed in brilliant oranges and reds, danced in the soft breeze that fall day.

"Thank you, Mama. A perfect way to end my week. It's been a little crazy, hasn't it?" I said, looking into her face.

"We both needed some calm, didn't we?" Mama said wistfully.

Once at the house, Mama began the evening ritual. After donning her traditional red and white apron, she went right to work on supper.

"Go on and practice now, Molly. It's a perfect time

before Father returns from the challenges of his day."

"Thank you," I responded as I headed to the living room.

I began with some basic exercises to maintain strength and dexterity. This must be why runners and skiers lifted weights to keep their muscles toned. I had never considered how playing the piano was like athletics before.

I felt a personal attachment to my piano though it was no match for Mr. Clancy's first-class grands. It wasn't just an instrument, but a family heirloom. It was first Mama's way back from when she was a little girl.

Inviting smells of freshly baked cookies soon wafted into the living room. Thank you, Lord, for a mother who makes our home a welcoming place. I felt contentment without even nibbling a cookie. Such delicious scents stirred even sweeter memories of days when we baked for the holidays together.

I heard the car on the gravel drive. Bracing for whatever might be my evening fate, I stopped playing and listened. The door burst open, followed by the sound of heavy steps. I felt my body tense up in anticipation. Father seemed more upset than he had been the night before. Oh, no. Not again. I went to the front entry to greet him, but he brushed past me. His behavior stirred my curiosity, and I followed.

It was apparent the aroma of fresh baking did nothing to provide relief from Father's problems. He had always noticed Mama's freshly baked chocolate chip cookies whenever he got a whiff. In fact, he usually snuck at least one before dinner. It was a family joke. Mama would always pretend-fuss over his violation of the "no sweets before dinner" rule with some chiding wrapped in love. Father often teased back that she would sure not want him to starve to death after his hard day at the office.

No joking this time. He was all business.

"Haven't you heard, Ruth?" Father said, waving the newspaper headlines in his hand.

Mama did not know what he was talking about.

"I think I will withdraw our money from the bank—now. While I can."

All of this commotion was before Father even washed his hands. Father was an accountant who made a steady income for our family. I didn't know how much he made, but we always had what was needed.

"Why would we need to take money out of the bank, Hank?" Mama queried.

"Because if the banks close like the financiers warn, our money will not be accessible. Maybe not ever again."

Father began slowly and softly, his voice escalating with intensity as he explained each point of his argument.

"Don't you see?" he added. "The banks can't stay in business if they lock all the dollars up in a building. They have to invest it to make money. If the investments go up in flames, then that source is gone. Forever. Imagine what would happen if everyone rushed to the bank to grab their savings at the same time."

"Come now." Mama coddled. "You need to calm down a bit. Then we can talk some more."

Here we go with the sacred suppertime show. It's called "Let's act like everything is fine so we can have a 'relaxing' meal together." It made no sense to me to live in this fantasy world.

"Let's sit down to a little baked chicken and mashed potatoes, Hank. Then you'll feel better," Mama encouraged.

We joined hands at the table, thanking God for our nourishing meal. Truly, that was the only normal thing about the evening. An unsettling silence distanced us, each left to our own reflections. The meddlesome clinking of silverware was the only interference in the lull. I thought how much we needed some spirit lifting music. Maybe it would at least relieve the obvious despair written on Father's face for a few moments. How can banks spend our money if we gave it to them for safekeeping? I didn't dare pursue that line of questioning.

Then I thought of an important question which might turn the tide of conversation. Father had planned to pick up the train tickets, so we wouldn't have to wait in line Saturday morning.

"Father, not to disturb you, but since we leave early in the morning for Detroit, did you pick up the tickets? This is such a dream-come-true for me. I thought I'd sleep with them under my pillow," I said, joking. I watched his face for a slight sign of humor.

"You two do not understand," Father said, bounding from his chair. "If the banks fail, it doesn't matter how beautifully you play the piano, Molly. Nobody will even have food for their bellies. Rich or poor. Everyone will be trying to survive. Who will have the money to afford a luxury like a concert?"

No longer feeling confident, I pleaded. "What are you saying? What about tomorrow?"

Mama looked stunned. She turned to face Father with his hands on his hips, and food barely touched.

"How much money do you want to take out?" she asked.

"Every penny. And I'm doing it tomorrow. If the banks close on us, we will lose everything we've worked so hard to save."

"Now you're scaring me, Hank."

"Father?" I was starting to feel queasy. "Are you going to

the bank before we take the train to Detroit?" I dared ask.

He ran his hands roughly through his hair.

"Sweet Molly, you don't understand! If our economy collapses like I think it may, there will be no symphony orchestra in Detroit or any other American city. Musicians have to be paid like everyone else. If there's a run on the banks, people won't spend one thin dime to hear an orchestra. Everyone will be clinging to whatever money they have," he spewed in a nonstop blast of verbiage.

Mama burst into tears and stood up, pale as a ghost.

"Father, what are you saying? We're still going tomorrow, right?" I responded, rising slowly from my chair.

We stood upright around the table like exclamation points, bodies proclaiming our intensity. Father reached over to take my hand and, in that instant, I knew. No tickets. Maybe, no audition.

"I did not, Molly. It did not cross my mind today. This is an impending crisis, dear. A CRISIS," he said almost shouting.

Father never shouted. I looked into his face and pulled my hand away.

"How can you be so mean, Father, to so easily dismiss all my work, my dreams? My future? Without a whisper of hope or even a prayer to God? You taught me faith, and this is what I get in a crisis?"

I sprang from the room, food untouched, and fled to the living room. In frustration and anger, I pounded the keys of Rachmaninoff's first eight chords like I was taught never to do. Striking the keys with an uncharacteristic force, I buried the sounds of the despairing voices. Buried them. I kept playing and playing and playing, drowning out the chaos.

Chapter 4—The Audition

I awakened with a start, realizing that it was The Day—the very day which had propelled me with purpose for months. My heart skipped a beat as I sat bolt upright. After months of practice, I knew I was ready to perform. I knew the cost, and the stakes were high.

As soon as such fervor captured my waking, an even deeper heaviness gripped me. The family blowout flashed like neon lights reminding me of demolished dreams. It would have been the most exciting day of my life if Father hadn't squelched everything. I peered out the window. What time was it anyway?

The black sky dotted with stars yielded no signs of dawn. Throwing my head back into the fluff of my feather pillow, its soggy wetness startled me. Ugh. I must have cried myself to sleep. In the chill of the night air, I yanked my blankets up close around me and shut my eyes again. Oh, God, please let me sleep. In truth, there was no urgent reason to get up. No audition.

"Molly," Father said while touching my arm gently.

I sat straight up again, shocked by the sight of Father sitting on the edge of my bed.

"What's wrong, Father?"

"Your mother and I made an important decision after you went to bed. You will go to the audition today."

"What about the crisis? The banks closing? The

symphony going broke?"

"I know," he said quietly. "Your mother and I talked it over. The truth is, our failing economy will still be in jeopardy whether you play today or not."

"Thank you, Father," I replied in a polite daughter tone. A lingering chill controlled my response.

He turned and quietly left my room. My heart was conflicted, dancing between gratefulness and anger. Why couldn't reason have prevailed the night before when Father so decimated my dreams? It did not make sense to me how a normal person could lose all reason.

I was not exactly a picture of grace as I rose from my sleepless night. Instead, I felt like I'd been running for hours. Running in place, going nowhere. My head spun with thoughts of the day's agenda as I brushed my teeth. Could I recover so quickly? After having the audition yanked from my hands and heart only hours ago, I needed to regain momentum.

Ignoring the harsh words from the previous evening, we rode in sleepy silence to the train station at 6:00 a.m. I thought we would never arrive, each slow second dragging into each sluggish minute. We were pretending again, of course. I wondered, is this kind of polite pretense what people call being socialized, or civilized?

As we got out of the car, Father took my hands in his and looked me in the eyes. My instincts were to pull away from his attempt to make up. I knew I had not forgiven him for the hurtful way he ripped away my hopes. Had he apologized? Not really. Where was God in this? Could we have prayed without all the lashing and slashing? Probably.

"Molly, you've worked with such great discipline. You

should be proud of yourself, no matter the outcome," he said. "We will have to leave the rest with the Lord."

He leaned down, kissed me on the forehead, and waved us off. I had to accept his actions as an apology. I always felt I was more of an accessory than a centerpiece in Father's life. I supposed that was normal, given how our family came together. After all, he wasn't really my father. My Papa died when I was four, and a few years later, Father fell in love with Mama. She is easy to love. I was a tiny appendage, but never the apple of his eye. No daddy's girl here. Yet sometimes he surprised me, and I needed to receive his effort in good faith.

Mama had already walked inside toward the ticket counter while Father presented his restitution speech. I was going to have to work on the necessary forgiveness part. Later. I ran to catch up with her as he drove away.

"Two round trip tickets to the Woodward Street Station, please," Mama announced with resolve.

We were finally off to do this thing we had been talking about for months and months. My attention plunged inward, and I walked toward a vacant bench in the waiting area. My mind was a midway with flashing lights, sounds, and ballyhoo clamoring for my attention.

All my lessons and hours of practice were about to be tested. The melody of the concerto danced in my head as I sat clutching copies of the music. I had to play from memory, but the judges used the written composition to check for accuracy.

What made me believe I would outperform all the other hopeful competitors? In reality, I probably couldn't. I knew that each candidate coveted this honor from the bottom of their toes to the tops of their heads. Slumping down on the hard bench, I threw my head back and closed my eyes. I had to let go of this turmoil. Time to concentrate on my role in this adventure.

Prayer. That's what I needed. The only words that came to mind were Help, Lord. I tried to calm myself. I even took a few deep breaths with Mr. Clancy's admonition in mind. Opening my eyes, I saw Mama seated beside me, waiting, as still as a mouse.

"All aboard! Train to downtown Detroit," the conductor called, interrupting my jumbled thoughts.

Jumping to my feet at his announcement, I spilled the music, scattering pages everywhere.

"Are you all right, dear?" Mama asked as she helped me gather the loose sheets.

"Of course," I said with unconvincing assurance.

We climbed aboard the train and settled into our seats. It crawled along the tracks, yet what a comforting sound. First the rhythmic clickety-clack, shortly followed by that familiar eerie sounding whistle as we accelerated. It was time for the audition, at long last.

"You've done a wonderful job of preparing for this opportunity, Molly," Mama said, patting my arm. "Now relax and enjoy your moment in the sun."

"I don't see any sun yet, Mother," I replied with a measure of cynicism. I could spout my negative thoughts to Mama. She understood.

Mama smiled back. She was forever the encourager, always the peacemaker.

"Remember. God will go with you wherever you go,

Molly. It's your job to invite him."

As I sat with my head back listening to the soothing sounds of the clattering train, the cacophony of my carnival-brain subsided at last. The ride didn't take long. In less than thirty minutes, the Grand Trunk Western chugged us right into the heart of Detroit.

After walking a block from the station to Orchestra Hall, I felt energized. Looking up, the towering stone columns beside enormous banks of windows made us seem diminutive. I walked forward to the massive doors, uncertain of my fate, but willing to explore like Alice in Wonderland. Heart pounding, I pulled on an oversized brass knob which would surely lead me to uncharted exploits. Maybe even the Queen of Hearts or the Mad Hatter would appear. I smiled at my inner musings, feeling playful like a child in my wonderment.

Once inside, my eyes surveyed the majesty of the hall, built only ten years ago. The lobby remained luxurious. Its oval shaped grand lobby ushered guests toward twelve steps up to seating in the main hall. Large, glowing lanterns stood guard on either side of the staircase. I could imagine myself gliding up the red carpeted stairs in a beautiful gown, sleek and fitted to perfection. Surely, this is a princess dream. What a glorious sight with the magnificent crystal chandelier above, twinkling like a million stars on a clear night.

After star gazing, I noticed the Young Artist registration booth and walked over to sign in. I heard a voice which yanked me back to the moment.

"Miss Martin, you're number nine on the audition roster today."

"May I practice somewhere before the audition, sir?"

"Yes, that has been arranged for you. Your practice time is between nine and nine-thirty in room twelve."

I swallowed hard realizing that this was the last chance for a warmup. Thirty minutes. Taking my performance number, I walked toward a long, velveteen settee in the lobby with Mama.

"How about some fresh apple for a snack?" Mama asked, pulling some apple slices from a small jar she'd stashed in her purse.

"I doubt anything would stay down, but thank you. I think I'd like to go listen to another contestant. Is that all right?" I asked.

"Of course. Whatever suits you best," Mama said in her soft-spoken voice. "I think it will be interesting to hear another student play as well."

The huge concert hall was dark except for the piano in center stage where I would soon perform. A circle of bright light flooded down from the balcony, encasing the concert grand's shiny ebony finish in a halo. As we entered, I once again felt Lilliputian, a tiny being lost in so grand a space. Mama and I tiptoed close enough to see the pianist while trying not to be a distraction.

As I settled into my seat, I noticed a small group of scholarly looking men in the front of the auditorium. They seemed to be taking notes. I realized they were the judges in charge of deciding the fate of this young musician. And, soon, they would determine my future as a musician as well. I wondered where each was from and what kinds of musicians they were. No doubt I had information like that in my packet somewhere. I tried to imagine their thoughts and wondered if they remembered ever being so young and eager.

At the judges' bidding, a young male pianist, then seated at the glistening grand, began running his fingers effortlessly up and down the keys. I closed my eyes to listen. He executed a demanding pattern of notes with ease. This contestant's talent was surely in his hands. The music sounded technically perfect. He was playing Mozart's 20th Piano Concerto in D minor, a masterpiece filled with musical fury from the heart of a different classical master. I recognized it from my studies with Mr. Clancy.

It seemed strange, though, because this student's rendition was so devoid of feeling. Mozart was transformed to a finger exercise, a drill from Hanon's Virtuoso Pianist study book. Often people quoted Beethoven as saying, "To play a wrong note is insignificant; to play without passion is inexcusable." I loved the emotional drama in music—it seemed unthinkable to omit the power of such emotion. The more I listened to this pianist, the more my confidence grew.

Glancing down at my watch, I realized that I only had ten minutes to find the practice room. This was the last chance to warm up my "personal instruments," as Father called my hands. I gestured to leave, and Mama understood. The contestant finished with a rising crescendo, and the sparse audience clapped politely. We exited in seconds.

"Mama, I only have a few minutes to find my practice room. Do you want to wait inside? Or would you like to stay here and read?" I asked while taking hurried steps toward the practice room. I must have had a funny expression because she appeared to be studying me.

"What would you like for me to do, Molly?"

Always thinking of others, Mama was willing to yield to my desires in that moment.

"Relax, Mama, and I'll be back in about thirty minutes. Continue to listen to the other performers, if you like."

We agreed on where to meet, and I scooted down the massive corridor to the catacombs of tiny rooms with upright pianos tucked in each of them. Thinking of Mama's loyal support, my mind raced back to a time when she was not there for me. The dark days of fears and loneliness in the Charity House were only rare flashbacks for me these days. Those years did make a formidable impression on me, but I refused to let them dictate who I was. No more. After my real Papa died, Mama had to leave me for a couple of years. She had no way to support me or care for me until she remarried.

As a little girl, Mama taught me Scripture for comfort. I knew God didn't want me to be afraid. His promises were to give me power, love, and even self-discipline like it says in Second Timothy. Over time, I learned to lean on God's perfect love, and Mama's imperfect, but comforting love. Even when she couldn't be there.

I peeked into several of the practice rooms and listened to some of the contestants practicing. I located my assigned room and began working my hands up and down from bass to treble and from treble to bass. My hands were cold and damp from perspiration. Nerves. I felt the anxiety. Back and forth I played, with runs, scales, chords, and arpeggios. I switched over to Rachmaninoff, but faltered several times at the very beginning of the concerto. Disgusted with my poor warmup, and feeling less than confident, I left the practice area to meet Mama. It was almost time anyway.

"Hi," I said as I approached. Mama was intently reading

one of her novels, completely absorbed in her own world of fiction.

"Oh, yes. It is about time for your audition, isn't it? By the way, this is such a good book, The Age of Innocence, it's called, by Edith Wharton. So interesting to see how the wealthy New Yorkers live," she said while rising to join me.

I nodded, acknowledging her remark, yet in my own world of distraction. We walked to the main hall at a fast clip and took seats in the back to wait for my number to be called.

"Number nine," the judge announced, glancing around the darkened, expansive auditorium. I popped up from my chair like somebody yanked my puppet strings from the heavens.

"Number nine," he called again with more force.

"Yes, sir," I said stepping forward with music in hand. I smiled.

"Do you have any questions before we begin?"

My mind was a vacuum. Empty of all cogent thought. I shook my head and answered, "No, sir."

"Your performance evaluation will be available at the booth in the lobby by mid-day," he stated in a most formal manner. "You may ascend the stage and begin when you're ready."

"Yes, sir," I answered, at least mustering proper decorum. Then looking into my eyes, the judge's face softened, if only for a moment. Maybe he did remember being my age. I could only hope.

The steps to the stage carried me behind a tall, velvet curtained area. As I stood in that dim enclosure, I hesitated before pulling back the heavy curtain and walking on stage. An unpleasant memory of those old orphanage days washed over my already vulnerable self. The darkness. The confinement. Dear God, NO. Not here. Not now. Please remove this oppression, in the name of Jesus.

I took a step forward toward the partition. I prayed again.

Dear God, take this moment and use it for something good, something beautiful. I know this spirit of fear is not of you.

With great determination, I parted the curtain, and proceeded to the spotlight in center stage. Mama said it was my hour in the sun. No matter what happened next, these next moments were mine to embrace. My new green knit dress, which accentuated my slender build, provided a sense of outer confidence. With a tenuous smile, I presented myself to the judges, my mother, and whoever else may have been seated in the darkness of that massive chamber.

By now my heart was thumping out of my chest. I had to take a long, deep breath to calm myself. I could not, absolutely could not, begin playing too fast. The pace would be untenable throughout the concerto and would likely propel me to calamity.

Slipping onto the black leather bench, I felt God's grace pour over me. Closing my eyes, the melody of this magnificent music poured into my being. I lifted my hands above the keys, poised to begin the dramatic opening chords. What a fitting prelude Rachmaninoff composed.

My fingers moved from the rich chords to the challenging runs, with fingers flying up and down the keyboard. I began to imagine how it would sound with the full symphony playing in accompaniment. Nothing else mattered in that moment. My soul drank in the depth of the music, and my hands responded to the keys as if they were one with the piano. Before I was consciously aware, I heard the thundering finale.

The passion of this Rachmaninoff concerto had overcome all else—all fears, all self-consciousness, all doubts. Above my loudly beating heart, I recognized another sound. It was the sound of vigorous applause from those who must have felt the inspiration as I had. Having poured out every fiber of my being, I stood in confidence that I had given it my all.

With the spotlight in my face, I could not see individuals in the darkness. As I descended the steps, on unsteady legs, I grabbed the handrail. In that moment, I saw the judges again, acknowledging how those few, highly esteemed men held my future. Would I launch as a professional musician in this venue, or was my aspiration a mere fantasy?

Chapter 5—Waiting

Mama sprang from her seat, making her way to the front as I approached the center aisle. Shamelessly, she threw her arms around me in the biggest hug. I was seventeen as we stood in this very public place, but at that moment, it didn't matter. I knew I was loved, and I knew Mama understood how important this audition was to me. No matter what the judges decided, whatever happened with the economy, music was my future, and I knew Mama was with me.

Mama stepped back to look into my eyes and said with a beaming smile, "I've never been prouder."

As we exited, we walked past the judges' table, and I glanced their way. I itched to know what they were writing on my evaluations. One white-haired judge peered over the top of his spectacles and nodded with a friendly expression. Another seemed deeply in thought. The third gentleman never broke his distinguished decorum, but glanced up to acknowledge me with a subtle smile. I knew they held the cards in their hands. They had the final say over my success as a potential concert pianist.

Waiting. Waiting. Waiting. Waiting to perform was difficult. Waiting for my evaluation removed any of the tiniest shreds of patience left in me. By now it was midday, so we were also growing hungry. Mama still had the sliced apple with her, aging now and tinged with brown. My tummy was growling, so I accepted it with gratitude.

Twice I'd been to the evaluation booth for my scores. The woman behind the counter looked sympathetic, but there were no results yet.

"If you're ready to eat now, I have a peanut butter sandwich for you," Mama said. She held up the sandwich wrapped with care in waxed paper like a gift. The ends were folded into triangles, but not taped down.

"This is enough for now," I said. "My tummy is in knots while I wait for my scores."

Thinking of all the famous composers and conductors who had stood right where I was, I gazed at the entrance of Symphony Hall again. I stood in awe. The famed Russian pianist Ossip Gabrilowitsch was the appointed Music Director of the Detroit Symphony. In fact, it was this conductor who refused to accept a position unless a new and suitable music hall was a part of his offer. Before that, the orchestra played at the old opera house. Thank you, Mr. Gabrilowitsch, for your powerful influence.

I strolled into the back corridors, peeking into the tiny windows of the practice rooms. To entertain myself, I analyzed the pianists who were making the most of their last rehearsal time, no doubt feeling nervous as I was. Their fingers raced up and down the keyboards with a good level of expertise.

Who were these young men and women? Was performance their life passion? Who would the judges select from among us all? Surely each performer must have carried secret dreams of success or they would not have achieved thus far. What kind or cruel fate would be mine?

After pondering my fate, I began the trek back to the evaluation booth again.

"Molly Martin," I said with boldness. "Number nine."

"Oh yes. I remember you. Let's see. No, it's not ready yet. I'm sorry."

I plopped down beside Mama on the velvet settee for a while longer, staring at the booth and waiting for a sign. Though we wouldn't learn who won the honor of performing with the symphony, contestants should receive their personal evaluations as soon as they were prepared.

Finally, after the minutes crawled by, the woman stood up and waved me over with a big smile. She acted like she knew who I was by that time. Best friends.

"Thank you," I said with gusto.

By now, I was so nervous my fingers trembled as I reached for the folded papers. I wanted to read the judges' analyses with my whole heart. But I did not want anyone to watch me. I surely didn't want to shed tears in public. That would be embarrassing. Everyone would know I had failed. Acting like a thief concealing my crime, I shoved the papers onto my stack of music so not to draw attention to myself. I strolled over to Mama as if I didn't have the results. She knew, of course.

"Mama, we can go now," I said.

"Aren't you going to read your scores?" she asked.

"Well. Yes. I will. But …"

"But what, Molly?"

I started to walk away from the evaluation area. At least at a distance, no one else could see my facial expressions. I desperately wanted to know what was written. What if my performance was not viewed by the judges in the way I experienced it? What if …? Oh, stop the agony. Open them up and read.

I slipped the evaluation papers from their hiding place. Fumbling a bit, I unfolded and then refolded them. When we were off by ourselves in the lobby, I opened them. At last, with trepidation. Glancing at the top front page, I saw the overall performance score was high: Technique—5/5, Rhythm—5/5, Tone—4/5, Memorization—5/5, Artistic Expression—5/5.

My smile could not be contained. I read the remarks penned at the bottom: "This performance displayed an intuitive understanding of Rachmaninoff's passion in Concerto #2 in C minor. This challenging piece was played with a musical depth unusual in a performer so young."

"Mama, Mama. It's all grand!"

Grinning like the Cheshire cat in Wonderland, my feet began to rise from the floor at a quickened pace.

"I'm ready now. Let's go home," I said buoyantly.

I nearly left Mama behind in my excitement as my feet skipped along.

"Molly, I am so happy for you. Here's to the beginning of your dreams," Mama said, lifting her arms high.

What I felt in my heart during the audition was confirmed. Mama took the paper from my hands, and began to squeal, only as Mama could.

"Molly, this is wonderful. You'll surely be chosen as the guest performer. Don't you agree?"

I smiled, but couldn't quite capture her optimism to believe I would be selected above the rest of the talent. That outcome would be left to God. I knew I had no control over it.

On the train ride home, Mama chattered about everything that had happened. I closed my eyes and smiled while she babbled on in her most inimitable way. The chugging rhythm of the wheels on the track accompanied Mama's soft voice. It was comforting to know she was beside me, especially in light of last night. Every now and then, I glanced at the changing landscape as we rolled along. Trees waved their bright red and gold leaves in a last hurrah before winter. White farmhouses dotted the fields, announcing a bold separation between the city and outlying commuter towns. My mind drifted. I had one overwhelming feeling—happiness. No regrets.

Jack wasn't there to hand me a bouquet with his handsome face smiling like in my dream. And no, Mr. Clancy was not able to hear the results of his years of investing in me. But at least that nightmarish dream with Mr. Hill holding his chemistry sign didn't come true.

I chuckled, thinking of all my previous expectations. Mama didn't even ask what I was giggling about. She had stopped reiterating the details of our experience, and her eyes were closed by that time. I imagined she was basking in the moment like I was. Sweet peace. As the train rolled toward our Royal Oak Station, the slowing of the train wheels awakened me from my tranquility.

"Congratulations," Father said as we disembarked. His eyes were weary, and the lines in his face were drawn tight. I could see he had forced the corners of his mouth to create a semblance of a sincere smile.

At first, I thought he was just being kind since he knew how hard I'd tried. Mama had called him from the station to tell him what time to meet us. I was sure she had carried on, the way she always did, sharing the best of our day with pride. I heard Father's voice, but didn't tune in with all my attention. Then, he repeated himself.

"Molly, did you hear me? They called about ten minutes before I left the house."

"Who? Who called?"

"The symphony conductor," he said. "You've been selected to play with the symphony, January 16!"

Father tried brightening his smile and opened his arms for a hug. A rarity.

"Congratulations to our young star," he added as he took Mama's arm and mine. We walked to the car arm in arm, looking a bit like Tweedle Dee and Tweedle Dum, plus one. We were united, for a change. I didn't grasp its significance then, but it was a memory I would need to hold in the future.

Tired, hungry, yet churning with energy from Father's announcement, I couldn't wait to get into the house. I had won! I thanked God for answering my prayers. My best was good enough. Or maybe that's not quite right. Maybe God poured the music through my hands. I knew he was able to do those kinds of things. At any rate, it felt glorious, and I was filled with thanksgiving.

First, I needed to get some food in my now grumbling belly. Next, I would call Winnie because I knew she would be thrilled. It's important to share our victories, especially since we always confide those aching-heart things. After downing a glass of milk and a peanut butter sandwich, I felt the weight of fatigue. I was spent. Emptied out like the glass I held. Only the filmy residue remained like the sweet memories lingering in my mind.

Diving onto the sofa before calling Winnie, I curled

up with one of Mama's softest handmade pillows. I heard Father whispering from the dining room. And, then Mama. I perked up to listen.

"Hush, Hank. Don't. Molly is exhausted, and she had such a wonderful day. Whatever this news, save it for another day, okay?"

As I was jarred from my half dozing state, I heard Father answer. "Ruth, we can't protect Molly forever."

"Shhhhhh, Hank. Go for a walk and cool down, if you must."

"It's time we all face what's happening. This is truly out of our hands," he countered, louder than a whisper.

The door clicked shut. He must have taken Mama's advice and gone outside. I heard Mama's footsteps coming closer. Pretending not to have overheard, my eyes remained tightly closed.

"Wake up, sweetie," Mama said shaking my shoulder. "Why don't you go on to bed now. You've had quite a day."

I wandered back to my bedroom, too tired to think, yet wondering what dreaded news Mama had postponed. Dear Lord, please take care of this problem while I try to sleep. Amen.

Chapter 6—A Roller Coaster Kind of Day

The whisperings of the unknown, and the potential of a new dreary fate eroded my own joyful spirit. As much as I wanted to ignore such foreboding thoughts, deep down, I knew. I, too, was vulnerable. Life's uncertainties were real.

I must admit that my mind wandered during the sermon that Sunday morning. However, I made some progress as I thought about everything. In that hour, I determined that I would refuse to allow these dark omens to suck life from me. Father could be as melancholy as he chose. I would refuse to participate. Instead, I would choose to live in the pride of my accomplishment.

I couldn't wait to get home from church Sunday. As soon as the old Packard came to a halt, I hopped out and whisked past Father and Mama to get inside.

"Mama, may I use the phone for a few minutes?" I called out. "I still need to tell Mr. Clancy and Winnie my good news."

"Of course, Molly. Please change out of your good clothes," she added. The mother reminder. Always. Goodness, I was nearly eighteen years old, not a child. Observing Mama's admonition with a nod and smile, I headed to my room.

I slipped off my silk stockings and Sunday dress. Of

course, I knew I shouldn't ruin them by lounging about the house, and lounge about is what I had in mind for those few precious hours. I selected my favorite flower print blouse, designed and sewn by Mama, and then slipped into my most comfortable brown skirt. Wooly knee-high socks would keep me warm. After I took time to unwind, chemistry now had my full attention.

I picked up the phone and scrunched my legs up on the small bench. To my surprise and glee, no one was on the line. I dialed Mr. Clancy's number, J5743. I rehearsed in my head what I would say while I listened to the ringing.

"Mr. Clancy? This is Molly Martin. I hope this is a good time for you. I have some wonderful news to share."

He had already guessed.

"Yes, it's true, Mr. Clancy. I so wish you could have been there. Despite my nerves, after I began playing, the music took command. There were only a few people in the room, but they all clapped enthusiastically. Except the judges, of course. I was left to imagine what they were thinking, which was hard."

"Oh, my child," he began. Then his voice got all crackly. He paused, and then cleared his throat.

"I'm so proud to have been able to work with you, Molly. My feet want to do a little jig right here and now. Can you imagine that?" He chuckled in his cute and funny way.

I giggled in response. "You're the bee's knees, Mr. Clancy. I can see you right now."

Then he covered the speaker and raised his voice. "Martha? Martha? Molly won!" he bellowed out to his dear wife.

"The judges were solemn folks, but one gave me a hint of a smile. Oh, how excruciating it was to wait for their evaluations," I said.

"It's true, Molly. Waiting after you have poured out your heart is awful, isn't it? I try to remember the contestants' feelings when I judge."

"I can't wait to share my scores with you," I added.

"Yes, yes, do bring the evaluations to your lesson. I'll see how to help you fine tune before the January concert. Congratulations, and thank you for letting me know."

Despite all the happiness from sharing my success, I felt depleted. Lethargic. I stretched out on my bed and almost drifted back to sleep. It was like I'd run an entire football field to score several touchdowns for the Chicago Cardinals. Not that I was much of an expert, but I heard the ball games when Father listened on the radio. Mr. Clancy always said that performing a concerto is akin to an athletic performance.

Rousing myself to share with Winnie, I was amazed to hear the call ring straight through to her house. As a rule, Sunday was a busy time on the party line.

"Winnie?" I said, hearing her voice on the other end. I didn't wait for even a second to see what she would say.

"I won! I won the audition. I really did. After I started to play, I felt like I was in that tremendous Orchestra Hall all by myself. Just me and that gorgeous Steinway grand. It was the most thrilling thing I've ever experienced."

"Congratulations, Molly! I can imagine you on stage right now. I cannot wait for you to tell me all the details, one by one. What did you wear? Oh, never mind. You already told me about your pretty knit dress." Winnie laughed and paused for one second. Then nonstop, like a river overflowing from the spring melt, she added, "How many people were there? What was the concert hall like? Were the judges nice?"

She stopped with a quickened breath. "Oh, boy. I can only imagine how boring school will be for you now."

School. Ahhh, yes. I would be a guest performer with the Detroit Symphony in January. Yet, somehow, I still had to get up tomorrow morning and sit through classes like every other student at Royal Oak High School.

"You have managed to thrust me back to reality," I said. "Here's a question. Do you think your parents would let you come over today?"

Winnie agreed to ask and called right back to say yes. Amazing grace again regarding the party line. I couldn't wait to see her. Since we hadn't done anything fun for a while, we agreed to reserve a few minutes for girl-talk. Winnie, always the organizer, delivered the ground rules.

"Just fifteen minutes for fun, and then we will work," Winnie reminded both of us. "Okay?"

I laughed at her taking charge, and nodded in agreement. She plopped down on my bed, ready to talk.

"All right, so give me some details," Winnie said.

"You should have seen Orchestra Hall," I began. "It is even more magnificent than the pictures—beautiful stone columns, celestial lanterns lighting the staircase, and the most breathtaking Steinway concert grand I've ever played. It was even better than Mr. Clancy's gem. Its pearl-smooth tones sang with every key stroke."

Winnie was so good at making me feel special. She listened to the beginning-to-end details of my victory.

Then, it was time to think about chemistry.

"Oh, Winnie. That Mr. Hill," I said, rolling my eyes.

"You know how he rocks up on the balls of his feet when he's upset?" she said, standing up to mimic his rocking motion. I laughed until tears spilled over. It felt wonderful to release my stifled emotions.

We could hardly stop giggling. It was good I didn't have Winnie in any important classes because she could make me laugh most anytime. We finally wound down, but before we talked chemistry, our conversation drifted. We had to talk about what girls love to talk about.

"Winnie, do you think you'll end up marrying Wally someday?"

"Hmmmm … that's a charming thought," she said, pausing to consider her answer. "I do think I'm in love with Wally. But, wait. Molly, I really have to get to tutoring you, you know? Now."

Ignoring her taskmaster voice, I pressed on. "Do you think a person learns to love someone?"

"Molly, stop it. Now you're diving into the deep. Love, really? What about the periodic table of elements? Or, gas laws and distinguishing among elements, compounds, and mixtures?" she scolded all the while laughing. Then, pausing, with a twinkle in her eyes, she let me go on.

"Or does love just come along with a bang, and you know it?" I asked.

"Are we talking about Jack now?"

"He's such a nice guy," I said, opening the textbook in front of me.

"I know he's fun. But, are you thrilled to the tips of your

toes when he looks at you?"

I smiled, remembering when Jack accidentally brushed up against me in the crowded hall. Was this the beginning of love? Or, a schoolgirl crush?

Glancing at the clock on my dresser, my stomach churned at the thought of how we'd squandered the time. The grandfather clock chimed the half hour. It was three-thirty already, so we swiftly moved on to chemistry. Or rather, we moved on to the essence of what I did not know about chemistry.

"Now down to work," Winnie pronounced most seriously. We dug into the textbook. Paper, pencils, memorizing tables, questions, answers, and problem-solving. It was two hours of book cracking, but it seemed only minutes when we heard Mama calling.

"Molly! Winnie's mother is here."

Our set-aside three hours had evaporated like dew on a summer morning. Yet, it was so worth it. I was certain Mr. Hill would be proud of me for making time for friends and normal things. Friends are important, he was quick to remind me. I had to laugh just thinking about him even remotely being proud of me.

I gave Winnie a quick thank-you hug goodbye, and she scooted out to her car. With its shortness of daylight, winter showed us her preview, and it wasn't even November. I hoped her mother could see me through the rainy darkness as I waved with an exaggerated swath overhead. I so loved Winnie's family. During our growing-up years, they invited me to their lake house for many summer weeks. They were like a second family to me.

After dinner, the phone rang while I was studying. I

heard Mama's footsteps approaching the phone cubby as I popped out of my room.

"Molly. It's for you."

Who could that be on a Sunday evening? Mama handed the receiver to me with "that look." Uh-oh.

"Hello. Oh, hi, Jack. Did you get my note last Friday?"

"Yes, thanks. How did everything go?" he asked.

"I won the audition," I said.

"Congratulations! I'd like to hear more," he replied. "Could we sit together at lunch tomorrow?"

"That would be nice," I said, trying to remain unflappable. After all, a girl has to play hard-to-get a little bit. Or so I thought.

Floating to my bedroom on the wings of infatuation, I felt my heart skip a beat, or maybe several. I sat down with my diary, ready to divulge my true feelings.

Dear Diary,

My life seems dreamy right now. I am certain of God's divine plan, and no matter what, I promise not to lose heart. With such promise of good things to come, tomorrow's small challenges seem surmountable.

I went on to bed with confidence and a million chemical formulas swirling in my head. Then, Monday morning arrived. The substantial clash between the ordinary me and the concert pianist me ensued.

My first class was Latin. Facing the task of translating Latin to English, my mind floated off the page in search of something more. I noticed the sounds of geese overhead flying toward winter warmth. I imagined being one of those birds, winging freely in the sky. I had to laugh. I wanted to flee these routine tasks with the geese. I was seventeen years old with a world of possibilities ahead of me, so why was I sitting here translating a dead language, for heaven's sake?

We began with class recitation, conjugating verbs, in unison. Oh my. The only positive thing I could say about such a boring exercise was, along with many others, we recited the word for LOVE in all its forms, singular and plural: amo, amas, amat, amamus, amatis, amant.

Remembering Mama's explanation of the virtues of Latin, I tried once again to put on some positivity. I looked around, wishing I had someone to confide in, or at least giggle with every now and then, fulfilling Mr. Hill's socialization goal for me. Analyzing the girls in my class, I saw no one who could relate to me. Many would marry their sweethearts soon after graduation, become housewives, and have babies. Their desires weren't in my dreams for a long, long time.

Before I knew it, the bell rang, and I was off to history. Two down now. I bumped into Meredith going into algebra class.

"Oh, hi, Molly," she said. "What have you been doing lately? I haven't seen much of you."

"Well, I've been busy. I competed in the Detroit Symphony's Young Artist Contest last Saturday, so, I had a lot of preparation."

"Oh, how nice," she said, glancing across the room. "Ta-ta, now. Good luck with everything," as she walked over to Joe. He was one of the Royal Oak football players.

Rah-rah, sis-boom-bah. I wondered if Meredith even understood what I was talking about. Why did I bother to tell her? I didn't want to boast, but my life had changed.

I knew God's purpose for my life, and it certainly seemed wasted while I sat in these irrelevant classes.

I heard the droning voice of my algebra teacher. My mind was elsewhere. At long last, the bell rang. Temporary freedom. I hurried toward the all-purpose room where we could take sack lunches if we couldn't make it home and back.

A familiar dimpled grin came into view as Jack popped out from the doorway of a now-emptying classroom. His sky-blue eyes and long, dark lashes always captured my attention.

"How about a spot of tea, My Lady?" he asked with feigned formality, extending his arm to me.

"Why, of course, Sir Jack." We laughed at our silly characterizations as we walked, linked at the elbows like a lord and his lady. Jack was always a kidder. Always quick to bring me a smile. We found a place to sit in the back and opened our sandwiches.

"I don't know if a lady should be dining on peanut butter," Lord Jack said.

"Well, what kind of lord eats bologna, anyway?" I quipped.

We ate and chatted about classes and teachers, all the usual, barely loud enough to be heard above the din of voices and the crackling of paper bags. Watching the clock had become paramount in the final ten minutes because I knew I must not be late for Mr. Hill's class. I certainly didn't want any extra attention from the professor.

Suddenly, Jack leaned in close enough that our shoulders touched. He looked directly into my eyes.

"Molly, I do want to hear about Saturday. Tell me. How

did it feel on stage with the judges studying your every move?"

I was momentarily speechless. I wanted Jack to know my innermost feelings, but this wasn't the place, and we certainly did not have the time. I nodded to affirm his question.

"Someday we'll have a quiet place to talk, and I can tell you everything," I replied.

Departing with a wave and exiting through different corridors, I was propelled to the science wing with one bit of extra bounce in my step that day. Perhaps, this could be what amo, amas, amat feels like. I was smiling, even entering my dreaded chemistry class. The stench of Mr. Hill's chemicals wafted into the hallway, a vivid reminder of my dratted temporary obstacles.

"Class, you will take the scheduled unit test on Wednesday. You may use your time in class today to review," Mr. Hill stated in his standard staccato speech. "If you have any questions, I'm here for you."

Mr. Hill was as passionate as a test tube. I studied this slightly balding man for a moment. Always in control. He wouldn't flinch if he discovered the pasteurization process and saved the world from deadly bacteria. I could imagine Louis Pasteur, upon his scientific breakthrough, jumping with joy over his accomplishment. But not Mr. Hill. Oh, no.

At first glance, I could see a host of problems on the study guide I didn't know how to solve. Unsettling. I tried some of the questions to appear industrious. After wrestling with the unsolvable, I decided to raise my hand. Mr. Hill leaned over my desk, studying my attempts.

"Oh, my," he muttered in disdain. He stood breathing his rank breath over me with little exasperated huffs and puffs.

"Who was your tutor, Molly? It's obvious you haven't grasped even the basics."

I could feel my embarrassment showing. Everyone nearby overheard his grumbling assessment. As an afterthought, I wondered why I'd bothered to ask him anything, allowing him justification to harass me again.

The bell rang, and I judiciously removed myself from Mr. Hill's proximity while he gave last minute directions. I was out of there with two classes to go.

At last, the school day ended. Relief. It began on such a positive note. But each class was another reminder of my dual existence. To a stranger, it would seem I was an average seventeen-year-old attending high school. Yet that was not real for me.

I left school relishing the memory of my few moments alone with Jack amid the throng. I noticed the dreary autumn sky and pulled my hat tighter over my ears. A mild melancholy draped itself around me. I began to hum my song. I was high and then I was low like the roller coaster at the beach in Chicago. I was so glad to arrive home, and with finality, I closed the door against the gusting wind.

"Hot cocoa?" Mama called to me.

"That would be nice. Whew. It's brisk out there."

Once safe and secure in our small home, I felt the chill of my dark mood ease away.

After sipping on the warm chocolatey goodness, I told Mama a few details about my day, except for the part about Jack. Father said he would be late coming home for dinner that night, and Winnie would be there by seven for more tutoring. I knew it was my time to practice.

In less than two weeks, I play the concerto with the symphony for the first time ever. It would be the only rehearsal we would have together prior to the concert. I couldn't let up practicing now simply because I won the audition. I was thankful that Mama allowed me grace to skip my kitchen chores, including setting the table. She prepared the evening meal while I worked, and just as I finished up, I heard Father's car pull into the driveway. Excellent timing.

"Hello, Father," I said, greeting him at the door.

He grunted an expressionless hello and brushed on past me.

Something was not right. Again. Father was normally cordial to me, even if not affectionate. During dinner, there was no usual talk of family, friends, and business. The familiar clink of silverware broke the heavy silence. Mama would initiate a question, and Father would respond in one-word responses. I said nothing. I was thankful no one asked me anything.

While clearing the table, I mentioned that Winifred would arrive shortly. Father's face strained even more, if that was possible.

"Ruth, do we have to be entertaining guests right now? It's a school night. I can't understand why everything always, always has to revolve around Molly's life," he announced with a raised voice, so uncharacteristic in our family. There was a sharpness, even an angry tone reverberating. Father pushed back from the table, and escaped to the living room like prey fleeing a predator.

"Molly, would you call Winifred now and tell her this is not a convenient time for her visit?"

"Mama! She's not coming for a social visit. She is coming to help me study for a test."

"I'm sorry, Molly. Tell her your father is not feeling well."

"I'm feeling just fine," Father bellowed into the dining room.

I looked at Mama, alarmed and humiliated. More than that, I was angry. I wanted to tell Father what I thought of his rude behavior. My tongue remained silent, but my thoughts flashed with a fierce rebellion. I knew the ground rules. Respectable daughters were never to provoke confrontations with their parental authorities.

I phoned Winnie right away. Someone was on the party line this time. Perfect. I went to my room and plunked myself down with the chemistry review. After a few minutes, I tried calling again. Time was slipping by, and Winnie would be arriving in a few more minutes. The phone remained unavailable, and alas, the doorbell rang.

"Oh, no, Mama. What am I to do?"

I opened the door and with relief saw the car was still there waiting for Winnie's safe entry. In a whisper, I tried to explain my plight.

"Winnie, I am so sorry. My Father is being unreasonable tonight, and he doesn't want any company. Maybe he's sick. That's what Mama told me to say."

"Oh, Molly, I'm so sorry. Reread the first two chapters, and then call me. Maybe I can coach you over the telephone," Winnie suggested.

"Yes, big if since I attempted to call you three times to cancel tonight."

Winnie ran back to her parents' car. I wonder what they would think about our family now. Father was not being fair, for sure.

I closed the front door, and stomped to my bedroom. I wanted Father to hear me. I knew this would be a long night, but I would try. I heard one ring of the phone, but it stopped quickly.

"Molly, you have five minutes," Mama called out. I could guess what that meant.

"Hello. Oh, Jack. It's nice to hear from you again," I said, trying to make my voice sound normal. "I have a major test tomorrow in chemistry so I can't talk now. I'm sorry. See you tomorrow?"

Inside, my heart was racing. Not from Jack calling, but from all the upheaval. I was thrilled that Jack called, but, why was Father acting so erratic? The pall of something-not-right hovered again. When would this cycle end?

Chapter 7—The Blessing of Completion

Test day. My head was pounding with anticipation of this high stakes test. For someone with no love for schooling, my sudden, but earnest desire seemed almost humorous. Of course, I realized Mr. Hill had prodded me with his high stakes curse. It certainly wasn't a burst in my enthusiasm for chemistry. No, this was about losing release time to study at the Conservatory.

Walking just ahead, I saw Winnie with some classmates on their way to lunch.

"Winnie," I called out, trying to catch her attention.

Winnie turned as I approached, and searched my anxious face.

"How are you, Winnie?" I asked, politely forcing a smile.

"Please, go on without me," Winnie said, waving her friends off.

"More to the point, how are you today, Molly?"

"My head is swimming. I know we didn't schedule this, but would you mind quizzing me once more before the test?"

My fingers were fidgeting as I waited for her answer. Winnie rolled her eyes, shook her head, and then giggled. Relief. She wasn't upset. Her soft auburn curls landed again, gently reframing her face.

"Of course. What are friends for? And, you know what else? I'll be as happy as you are when this chemistry test is over."

Winnie's radiant green eyes were compassionate, as she led me by the arm out of ROHS that day. Walking together to the soda fountain, we pretended we had no pressing matters that day, if only for those few precious moments.

"You are a picture of autumn, Winnie. I really love your brown and orange plaid wool skirt. Is it new? And it goes so well with your hair."

"Thank you. My grandma gave it to me for my birthday. I was admiring your new scarf too," she answered, glancing my way.

"Thanks. I'll be sure to tell Mama. It's a pretty shade of red, isn't it?"

Best friends. Girl talk. Small talk.

We slipped into our favorite booth in the corner where we hoped for a bit of privacy, if possible.

"What can I get for you two?" the waitress asked.

We each pulled one nickel out of our coin purses and plopped them on the table.

"Root beer, please," we said in unison. The waitress laughed as we did.

It was frothy and foamy on top, sweet and cold on the bottom. Yum. Winnie pulled half of her bologna sandwich slowly out of her paper bag, trying to conceal it from the fountain manager's eyes.

"Where's your lunch?" Winnie asked.

"I have a kaleidoscope of butterflies flitting in my tummy, Winnie. I didn't even bother to bring any food today."

"I'm not sure skipping meals is a smart move, Molly. You need that brain of yours functioning in tiptop shape, you know?"

Between bites, Winnie went on with her chatter.

"Have you heard that Irene made up with Don again?" she asked.

"Oh, poor thing. She can have him if you ask me. You can't trust him. He's always flirting with anyone who will give him a look."

"Poor Irene. I hope she doesn't dive too far into this relationship. I wouldn't want her to get hurt by Mr. All-About-Me-Donald. Okay, let's do your review questions, Molly. On the way back to school, I'll tell you about a party idea I have."

"Ooooh, fun. I can't wait to hear more," I said.

We reviewed all we possibly could in twenty-three minutes. At least, I finally had memorized the basic symbols and formulas. Only God knew if I would figure out how to use them on the test.

As we began the walk back to school, our conversation returned to other important considerations. At least, considerations which were important to us.

"Winnie, I think I might really be falling for Jack," I confessed.

"You mean falling in love with him?" Winnie asked.

"Maybe. He seems so interested in what is important to me."

Winnie nodded. "Of course, I agree. Jack seems to care about who you are."

We walked along, our feet shuffling through the leaves as the question of love hung in the fall air.

"So, about my weekend idea, Molly. What would you think if we had a masquerade party?"

"Oh, that sounds marvelous! Who do you plan to invite?"

"I think I'll ask Irene, Don, Ruth, Fred, Wally—and you, of course. We'll probably play some music. And, that means we'll be dancing too," she added with a wink.

"I would love to come."

"So, here we go with the big question. Do you want me to invite Jack too?"

She was smiling, with that knowing kind of look. Without a word spoken from my mouth, I grinned back.

"It's settled then. I'll ask Jack," she said.

I marched into science like a soldier facing enemy fire. I took my seat, the second one in the third row back. Mr. Hill had us sit in alphabetical order so he could remember our names. I was "M" for Miss Martin. That was Father's name, and even though he hadn't legally adopted me, I used his name at school. I was thankful I was in the back whether Molly Martin, or Molly Ruthven. Happy to be as far from Mr. Bunsen Burner as possible.

"Begin immediately," Mr. Hill said in his usual, joyless intonation. He passed test papers from the front to the back. There was a quick rustle of paper and pencils, followed by purposeful silence. I peered up from my test paper, watching my classmates begin. Not everyone looked confident, but they were all busy, nonetheless. Then, there was poor Larry Phillips seated next to me. He flipped through the pages, and then sat looking dejected. He looked even more miserable than I was.

Dear God—don't let me end up like Larry. Help me figure out this work and please help poor Larry too. He never seems to get anything right. I carefully penciled in the date at the top of the page: October 29, 1929. I had prepared myself the best way I knew how, considering my slow start and lagging interest. Now please let everything come together, Lord. Plunging into the matter before me, I started in earnest. One by one, I tackled the problems with all I had.

Formulas were dancing around in my head, making a great commotion. However, they needed to pick up their pace. Maybe the formulas were gracefully doing some ballet pliés, but I needed some ragtime going on. I giggled at my silly personification. Stop distracting yourself, Molly. Concentrate.

The sounds of students' pencils scooting along the papers provided a warning shot. It accentuated my slowness in this race against the bell. My tension rose as I analyzed the next unanswered problem. The bell rang, jolting me like lightning. No, not yet. Not now. I was not finished.

"Please hand in your papers when you leave," Mr. Hill announced.

I approached Mr. Hill, hands trembling, test paper shaking. "Sir, I still have six problems to complete. Would it be possible for me to finish them after school?" I asked.

"No, Molly. You have no more time than anyone else," he said firmly.

"Yes, sir."

I walked out of chemistry defeated. But, on the bright side, the test was now out of my hands. Jack waited for me at my locker after school. He handed me a note with one of his hand-drawn comic characters on the front.

"This is me waiting for you," he said. The drawing's face was predominately an enormous toothy grin. It did turn my own frowny countenance around.

"I love to make you laugh," Jack said, as I stood giggling at his caricature.

"So, Winnie is throwing a party Saturday night. Are you going?" Jack asked.

"I think so. I haven't asked yet, but I'm hopeful."

He leaned forward, his forehead almost touching mine. "I will be the one disguised as a maestro. Will you be my concert pianist?" he said in a mysterious voice.

"I will be most delighted to play a concerto with your symphony, charming Maestro," I replied. I tried to laugh in a carefree way, but could feel the blood rushing to my face.

As we left school on that Indian summer afternoon, Jack walked the first three blocks carrying my books.

"What was the most wonderful part of your audition?" Jack asked. His questions were always so caring.

When we parted, Jack continued straight where I turned right toward our bungalow. After he was well out of sight, I skipped and twirled along the sidewalk, bouncing along like a first grader. I couldn't wait for the weekend, and the concert in January. Today was only Tuesday, but so many good things were happening. I could hardly keep my emotions tucked inside. Well, I guess I actually didn't. I looked around to see who may have been watching, and laughed. From several doors away, I saw Mama sweeping the front porch.

"Hello, Mama," I sang out.

She looked up and waved.

"Well, I can tell you had a lovely day, Molly. Come in for a little snack, and tell me what's making you so happy, dear."

"Since the weather is so pleasant, let's sit out here, Mama."

She set the broom aside, and we sat down together. For a long minute or two there was just the squeaking of the metal glider and the whisper of late fall breezes. I was grateful to have Mama there beside me even without sharing my heart. I couldn't tell her the giddiness I'd felt when Jack made me laugh, and I certainly couldn't tell her my drama in chemistry.

Finally, I asked. "Mama, Winnie is having a masquerade party. May I go? It's Saturday evening."

"I'll check with your father, but it should be all right."

"I think Jack is going too," I said, staring straight ahead.

"Hmmm. I think you must care about this young man," she said with interest.

I turned and smiled at her. I didn't have the right words to describe my feelings about Jack, especially to Mama. My emotions were so new, and I really wasn't sure what to think myself. Love was in direct contradiction with my immediate future.

The warm sun soon disappeared, sinking behind the tall oaks lining our street. The gentle breeze now delivered chills instead of peace. I shivered, and Mama wrapped her arm around me. In just a few minutes, it would be dark and cold, a trick of fall days turning to night. In unison, Mama and I gathered our things without a word. It was time to work on supper before Father arrived. Would tonight be peaceful like the gentle breeze—or cold as nightfall? Should I brace for more trouble, or place my trust in God?

Chapter 8—"Extra, Extra, Read All About It!"

I heard the familiar sounds of our Packard rolling into the driveway. Then the front door creaked. I prayed. I yearned to see Father stroll in with a grateful smile after whiffing Mama's most favored vegetable soup. But I steeled up for whatever might be brewing.

I smiled in hopefulness as Mama pushed open the café doors.

"Here, here, Hank. Let me take your coat," she said giving Father a welcoming kiss on the cheek.

She helped lift Father's coat from his drooping shoulders and studied him as she hung it on the coat rack. Father seemed agitated again. No, he looked more like someone died. What now? I hoped this was not another disruption to our normal calm.

"Thanks," Father uttered with effort.

His answer was barely audible from the kitchen where I busied myself by stirring the soup.

"Did you have another unpleasant day, Hank?" Mama asked.

This time his voice grew more robust—vehement, in fact.

"You haven't heard, Ruth? It's been in the headlines, on the radio …"

He seemed frustrated as to why Mama didn't know what everyone else knew.

"No, Hank. I've been right here cleaning," she said with a childlike innocence.

"What in the world is going on?" I asked.

At that, Mama waved at me to begin dishing up supper as they walked toward the living room. I could feel the tension rise, but went about checking the biscuits. This would normally be the perfect comfort food accompanied by Father's favorite blueberry preserves. But, tonight? Probably not. Father's voice escalated again.

"I don't know how we will be able to pay for the house," Father said. His voice broke.

I couldn't hear Mama's whispered answers. I moved closer to eavesdrop. Then—silence. Then—footsteps.

Abruptly, both parents pressed against the café door at once, almost slamming into me. I jumped. I'm sure I had a "Who me?" look on my face. Father's flushed face was tight, like an overfilled balloon. It would only take one gentle prick, and "Whoosh!"

"It's time to eat supper," Mama announced.

Her worried eyes contradicted her calm voice as she began carrying in the soup. We all knew Mama's ways, especially at suppertime. One thing our family always did was have a family supper and polite conversation. If Mama couldn't iron out a problem, she maintained a pretense of normalcy, at least for this sacred hour. However, this was different. Yet, with great predictability, after giving thanks, the play acting began.

"Hank, how is the car running now the temperatures have dropped?"

"It's slow to start in the mornings, and of course, after work when it's been sitting outside. It's too bad we don't have a garage. I wish we had built one years ago," Father answered.

Father was tight-lipped, but he went through the motions. I could tell he was miserable in his pretend role. Sometimes I chimed in, still searching for clues. I wanted to blurt out, "What's going on anyway?" I knew better. During supper, we had to put our heads in the sand like an ostrich family. The charade seemed daffy to me. I prayed the problem would slip away. I imagined it slinking into the darkness, never to return. Hope upon hope, even crossing my fingers like a little girl, I tried to think "on the sunny side," like the popular song. Then, changing topics, Father suddenly turned his attention to me.

"Molly, have you heard the Farmer's Almanac's weather predictions? Even for Michigan, they're expecting wicked lows. The dangerous kind of cold."

"That sounds dreadful for our usual ice-skating fun," I answered, playing along with their silly game.

This foolish conversation reminded me of the old fable about the man in the museum who noticed every little detail, but missed the big-as-life elephant. I could see we had an elephant sitting in the middle of our table, yet I was forbidden to mention it.

The conversation seemed to wither there, and I was grateful. Silverware clinked once again, and we ate in quiet isolation. Thinking of a freezing winter ahead, I distracted myself with my own daydreams. After skating, Jack and I could sip hot chocolate and snuggle by the fire at the city park. Maybe this could be a wonderful winter, bitter cold or not.

Mama had relieved me from dish duty that week, so after what felt like a tortuous eternity, I asked to be excused.

"Of course, dear," Mama answered.

I felt sure she wanted Father to herself to hash things out anyway. So be it. Since I was the last to learn what this was all about, I decided to pretend nothing was wrong as well. If they could, I could.

As I walked to the piano, I decided to pick out familiar music I had studied over the year. It was relaxing to play whatever my heart desired without attention to the concerto. I needed to keep my fingers in training, and that was the important task. I chose some lighthearted pieces which would also lift my spirits. Father might even feel better. Ahhh, a Mozart Sonata collection would be perfect for the evening. After a time, I glanced over to the mantel clock, and realized I had already spent two hours at the piano. I had so enjoyed playing, it seemed like no time had passed. I forced myself to stop.

In the abrupt silence, I heard a quiet sobbing from my parents' bedroom. I didn't see Father anywhere. Tiptoeing to their door, I leaned close to listen. Maybe I would figure out what was going on.

"It's all over the country, Ruth. There's not a thing I can do about it."

"What do you think will happen to your company, Hank?"

Father's answer was muffled. Every ounce of me wanted to barge in and say, "If there's a tragedy here, let me in on it!" But I was well-aware of what kind of trouble I'd be in if they found me snooping. I scooted to my room. If it was serious enough to upset them, then I should know too.

After all, I was no longer a child.

I had some homework to do, no matter the unsettled feeling. Before I started, I opened my Bible. Lord, help me find some peace in this confusion. I started reading and found just what I needed. Joshua 1:9 jumped off the page. Okay, God. I want to be strong and courageous. Hmmm. I'll try my best, but I need you to be right here beside me like you promised. Back to work again. I must concentrate on what seemed less relevant, but was essential homework.

Very early the next morning, I heard Father leave. At breakfast, Mama's eyes were red and swollen from her tears. She pretended nothing was wrong. After eating a bowl of Corn Flakes, I scooped up my books to leave.

"Bye, Mama. I hope you can get some rest today," I said as I left for school.

"I pray you'll have a God-blessed day, Molly," she replied with a faint smile.

Latin class continued with its usual translation exercises followed by a pop quiz. But when I walked into history class, last night's mystery was unveiled in enormous letters. Mr. Wolter had the news headlines plastered up on the chalkboard. BLACK TUESDAY: THE MARKET CRASHES.

"Ladies and gentlemen of Royal Oak High School," he began. "Life as you know has changed … as of yesterday. Our economy is in a precarious condition. The United States of America is in trouble financially."

Good grief. He sounded like he was the president or something. Hands shot up with questions from across the room.

"What caused the market to drop so fast?" Jerry asked.

"If we understood all the causes, this probably wouldn't have happened," Mr. Wolter replied. "We've actually had a week's worth of falling market prices, Jerry. Many people started selling their stocks because they were afraid. It's like getting on a slide. Once you start down, it's very hard to stop the ride."

As Mr. Wolter talked, I understood why my father had been so upset. I still couldn't understand how this would affect me in any tangible way. Nonetheless, it seemed serious since people were talking about businesses and banks closing. Why would a bank close? I still couldn't wrap my head around that. How could it close with all our money inside?

I was just thankful I was not a little girl in a children's home. Father would likely not have wanted to take on a wife and child, especially if his job was in jeopardy. Mama wouldn't have been able to come for me.

The other day, Mama told Jayne at the Beauty Shop that President Hoover would not let things get too bad. After all, that's what presidents are for. I prayed she was right.

In chemistry, Mr. Hill continued teaching as if nothing were new in his life, or ours. Of course, I should have expected that. I promised myself I would study chemistry with diligence. Mr. Hill was no force to reckon with, and he held the power card. Certainly, I did not. I amused myself with how ironic it would be if I became one of his top chemistry students. That would be a real opinion changer for Mr. Hill, now wouldn't it, I thought, stifling an inner giggle.

"Students, your tests will be returned to you on Friday after grades have been entered," he announced.

Whew, I was relieved that I didn't have to think about that for another two days. Winnie and I met after school at my locker, as we often did.

"Molly," she said, giving me a big hug.

"Are you all right?" I asked.

"I'm okay. Are you worried?"

"Not really. We'll be okay," I said, sounding confident. "Remember, God promises to be with us. So, we can stay strong and courageous, right?"

"Sure, Molly. The end of the world as we know it has not arrived," she replied with a quiet chuckle. "And, my parents said I could still have the party this weekend. Are you able to come?"

"Oh, my. I completely forgot about it. Father was so distressed last night that I didn't bring it up. Mama was going to ask him, but then I heard her crying in the bedroom. I'll see if I can find a calm moment to ask tonight."

That afternoon, Father was already home when I came in. He didn't acknowledge my arrival, but remained glued to the newspaper. The house was so quiet, it felt creepy, but I liked it better than all the angst. Mama was putting together a supper of leftovers with the big pot of soup from last night.

"How was your day?" she asked as usual.

"Mama, now I know why you were so upset last night. You could have told me instead of pretending there was nothing wrong. I'm not a little girl anymore, you know?"

Her eyes were fixed on me as I explained what I knew about Black Tuesday.

"But, Mama, the Lord reminded me of our strength in

him when I read Joshua 1:9. I didn't even know what was wrong, but he promised he would be with us."

"We will need that added dose of strength, Molly. I'm thankful you were encouraged."

At supper, Mama prayed. "Lord, please help us with all our needs, and help those who are losing their jobs. Thank you for our home that keeps us warm and food to keep us healthy. Amen."

"Father, the Black Tuesday news was all over our school today. I'm sorry you felt you had to face this alone. But you have a job, so we are thankful for that," I said, trying to add a positive note.

Father looked at me with a weary kind of smile. I was grateful he was calm.

"Thank you, Molly," Father replied.

"Changing the subject, Father, will it be all right for me to go to Winnie's party Saturday night? Her parents said she could still have it, even with the economic muddle," I said.

"Oh, yes, Hank, I forgot to mention it to you last night," Mama added.

"I think it would be a good idea for you young folks to enjoy a get-together," Father said. "No point in everyone being glum. I will do that for all of us."

He tried to chuckle, but it didn't sound genuine.

"Father, is there something you need to say?" I asked.

"Well, Molly, I don't have any really good news. I don't know how this latest development is going to affect us. Since I am the accountant for my company, I may be safe from the job cuts. Guess somebody has to keep the books even in the bad times."

I felt better just hearing Father talk about it. Life felt normal again for those moments of sharing. Had the tempest passed us by? After dinner, I practiced, did my homework, and wrote a short note to Jack. Then, I took a few minutes to write in my diary.

> Dear Diary,
>
> I've been too busy to write lately. So, to catch up, I'll tell you about Saturday night. It's only three days away, and it should be loads of fun. Overall, I'm happy with the way things are going in my life. Jack is coming to Winnie's too, and I know we will have a grand time together. I can't believe what all is happening. First, my audition victory, and now it feels like I could be falling in love. Of course, nothing serious for now, but I've already told you all that. One dreamy thing seems to follow another, Diary. I am a grateful girl. Goodnight for now.

As I fell into bed, I knew my heart wasn't filled with joy over the way things were going in my life. Some exciting things were happening. I knew life might have seemed normal for a few moments, but in honest revelation to myself and God, I still felt the uneasiness. What I wrote in my diary was a parallel universe to my existing truth. I realized I had pretended just like Mama at suppertime. I often wrote my heartfelt thoughts in my diary, except now that wasn't quite true. Life was strange. How could it be so good on one level while my future was hanging in the balance?

And please, God, watch over my parents. They have the worry of Black Tuesday and where it will lead. They need you to get through this. And, I might too.

Chapter 9—Is This Love?

Friday. A new day arrived right on time, and I was so happy to see it. We were all relieved, considering the impact of the devastating news for all our families. One last day of school in the week, and then Winnie's party. Something fun for a change, and I couldn't wait.

In chemistry, good old Mr. Hill announced that he had finished grading our tests. What a way to upset the apple cart, I'd say. I wished he had waited until Monday instead of ruining my perfect weekend.

As we gathered up our belongings, The Professor, as we called him behind his back, placed the tests on each desk, face down, centered with precision. His pace increased as he went through the rows, making sure each student had their paper before the bell. He paused for one second when he got to me. Looking down over the top of his spectacles, he paused, tapped the test paper, and gave me that look. You know the kind of look. The one that says you didn't make it. If only he had put it down and kept going, but no. He had to make a scene with everyone else around watching. I didn't have the heart to even look at it, so I folded it in half and placed it in my notebook.

After the last bell, Winnie joined me at my locker with a joyous smile and sparkling eyes.

"Molly, are you ready for a party this weekend? I am," she said.

"Yes!" I answered enthusiastically. "But then, there is this."

I pulled the folded test from my notebook, shaking it open between the two of us. I sighed. In large numerals at the top, Mr. Hill had penned an obscene sixty percent in red.

Winnie's eyes widened as she absorbed the news. She had probably never ever gotten such a low grade in her whole life.

"Oh, Molly, I know you can do it if you work hard from now on."

I shrugged with uncertainty.

"Look, Winnie. I'm rehearsing with the symphony in less than two weeks. Do you really think I'm going to spend hours and hours on this chemistry class?"

"Do you think your parents will be upset?" Winnie asked.

"Right now, I need to pretend everything is fine. I don't want to ruffle them this weekend when Father is already so distressed. Anyway, my parents are really good at acting like everything is all right." That comment made me snicker even though pretense was not my friend.

"Let's get out of here," Winnie replied with resignation. "We have to work on the party."

"Molly and Winnie, two of my favorite people at Royal Oak High," Jack said, approaching us with his usual smile. "Are we still partying Saturday?"

"Sure. It's still on," Winnie replied. "Be at my house at seven o'clock."

"I can't wait," I said peering into Jack's twinkling eyes.

The three of us walked out of school arm in arm with Jack in the middle. How special to have good friends. They mattered more than anything, except for music.

Tomorrow I would have fun for a change, and chemistry would take a backseat. I will wrestle with that obstacle later. Or as Mama would say, "mañana—tomorrow, tomorrow. Or, maybe the next mañana, or the next. Anyway, I knew chemistry should not ruin my weekend.

"What are you wearing to the party, Winnie?" I asked.

"Since it is a masquerade, I'll surprise you."

"Okay. I'll see if I can figure out which one you are," I said laughing. "Maybe you'll be the one who opens the door?"

That afternoon after school, Mama brought out her grab bag of scrap material.

"Let's see, Molly. I should still have some satin material in here left over from that dance costume I sewed a few years ago. I can whip up a mask if you'd like, since the party is tomorrow. Does your old costume still fit?"

I had taken dance lessons for a while, but I really didn't have the time to pursue it in high school. Fortunately, I hadn't grown that much, either taller or wider. I was still the beanpole I was when I was thirteen or fourteen, which came in handy for one's wardrobe.

"I haven't tried it on yet, but I will after I practice," I answered. "I don't want to disturb Father's peace with my 'thundering chords,' as he calls them."

Chuckling to myself about Father's description, I dove into the piano keys with finger exercises, and then went straight to the introduction of the Rachmaninoff concerto. Oh, how I loved the sound of those 'thundering chords.' I needed to play other music as Mr. Clancy suggested, but I also couldn't lose touch on the most important piece of my lifetime.

Much to my relief, dinner was calm and quiet that night. Father didn't talk much, but he seemed to be trying. I helped Mama with the dishes and then dug out my old costume. Without that, I didn't know how I would masquerade. As a last resort, I could always dress like a hobo. When I was growing up, we were all "hobos" when we had nothing else. Mama had worked so hard to make each of my dance costumes. For this one, she hand-sewed three layers of gauze over a skirt of white satin. I danced into the living room, swirling around to make the gauze float in the air making Mama smile. A nice change.

"Well, aren't you the princess," Father said looking up over the top of his newspaper in his specs.

I laughed. "It fits, Mama. There are some advantages to being skinny."

She smiled with admiration, and handed me her completed handcrafted mask.

"Perfect, Mama. I know nobody will recognize me now," I said jesting.

We all laughed. The darkness of the world could not shatter our simple joy. It was time for some music, singing, dancing, and laughing with friends. Saturday evening couldn't arrive fast enough. And, at last, it did.

As soon as I walked into Winnie's parlor on Saturday, my eyes spied a sophisticated looking "knight" wearing a gold belted white tunic. Of course, he wore a mask too, but nothing could disguise Jack's brilliant blues. He surprised me by not dressing up like a maestro, but he probably didn't own a suit.

"So, who do you think I am, Sir Galahad?" I asked. I surprised him with a quick pirouette followed by a curtsy.

"Hmmm. Let me see you do that again," Jack said.

Jack knelt on one knee in a pose most suitable for a knight, and reached for my hand.

"Oh, Milady, you are my one and only."

There he was again, acting silly like he loved to do. Giggling at our own antics, we went off together to see the other costumes. Before long, the disguises came off, and the music began. First, we tuned in the radio to find dance music, but after a few minutes, one of the evening story dramas came on.

Winnie's parents had a Victrola phonograph machine, but only a few records. Because they were expensive. Victrolas were not usually affordable for the average family. Owning one was a privilege. After dancing to those songs until we were bored, requests began.

"Maybe Molly will play for us. Will you, Molly? Please, please?"

Winnie asked first and then soon, the others chimed in.

"Yes," pleaded Irene.

Everybody cheered when I finally took my place at the piano. While playing some favorite tunes, including the new and jazzy "Charleston," I watched the happiness from my piano bench perch. Everybody having a grand time. Then it dawned on me how much fun everybody was having, except me. For once, I didn't want to be alone at the piano. I wanted to dance with my friends.

Jack and Winnie were doing the Charleston together,

having many laughs. Winnie's boyfriend, Wally, hadn't figured out this new dance so he was on the sidelines. Actually, Wally was sort of a gangly, long-legged guy, so she borrowed Jack. At last, Jack pulled up a chair and sat beside me, breathing hard after the Charleston kicks and twists.

I switched the pace, playing some slower, more romantic favorites: "I Want To Be Loved By You" and "If I Could Be With You One Hour Tonight." It seemed like just minutes before Winnie's mother came in to say it was time to end the party. Where had the time gone?

When I started playing "Everybody Loves My Baby," Jack slid over beside me on the piano bench. Everyone started singing the lyrics together: "Everybody loves my baby, but my baby don't love nobody but me, nobody but me, yes."

It was marvelous having Jack next to me with his arm placed around my waist, gentle as a dove. It wasn't a dance marathon for me, but at that moment, my heart was full.

Was I falling in love? Was my crush turning into the real McCoy? Maybe I shouldn't be so mean about girls wanting to get married when they graduated. I recognized how special these emotions were. They were all new to this single-minded, slightly driven musician type.

Since I was spending the night, I was still there when Jack said his goodbyes. Near the front door, Jack pulled me near and kissed me gently on the forehead. Right in front of everybody. It was brief, but oh, so wonderful and tender. I wanted Jack to hold me forever, but I had to let him go. Jack's cologne lingered on my costume as a sweet reminder of his embrace. These would be sweet memories to store for less-than-happy days.

Was Jack a part of my future, or were my feelings a passing fancy? One thing I knew for sure. Jack would never take first place above my desire to become a professional musician. That was number one in my book.

Chapter 10—"I Will Not!"

Two Weeks Later

Why was Father home early again? I noticed the car in the driveway, but it was way before our usual suppertime. I had hoped to rehearse before he arrived. Please, Lord, no more battles. This was not how things were supposed to work. Maybe Father had no job. No, surely that wasn't it. He was an accountant, and that made his job more secure. He said so just the other day.

"Hello, Father," I said, noticing he was pacing back and forth like a starving lion.

"What a nice surprise to see you before supper," I said, feeling most insincere.

"I'm home, Mama," I said, raising my voice to reach wherever she was.

Then, looking into Father's face I noticed his now-familiar scowl. If only President Hoover would just do what presidents are supposed to do, I'd have a much nicer father again. What was taking so long to fix this situation?

It had been nearly three weeks since the stock market failed. Now some of the banks were closing just as Father predicted. People could not even get their own money out, which really confused me. I was astonished, in fact. How could a bank refuse to give you your money? Where was the money if the bank didn't have it? I clearly didn't understand this kind of robbery.

I needed to practice for my sole rehearsal with the symphony Saturday, so I knew my next question would be awkward. "Father, I don't want to disturb you, but I really must practice today."

He nodded his head to acknowledge my request. I walked toward the kitchen to find Mama, who hadn't yet appeared on the scene. About that time, Father decided to stretch out on the rose-colored sofa. Guess he grew tired of his endless parading. So, where did he plop? In the living room where the piano sat. Why there? I knew he would become agitated when I started practicing.

"Mama? What is going on? It's not like Father to be home at this time."

Mama was wearing her brightly checked apron as she stirred the macaroni and cheese casserole for supper. Tears streaked her cheeks.

"And you? What's the matter? Mama, what is wrong now?"

Her swollen eyes looked into mine with pain brimming over her lids in tearful streams.

"What is happening to our family?" I asked again, raising my voice. I needed a straight answer, and no one was giving it.

Before Mama said one word, Father's tall frame burst through the swinging doors. His slightly graying hair was tussled from his hands raking through it. His shoulders were hunched like a prizefighter. Who was this madman?

"Don't speak to your mother in that tone, young lady. She has enough on her mind without having to defend me."

I was startled, and equally perturbed at his vehement attack.

"I'm sorry, Father. What am I to think? Something is seriously wrong around here when Mama is crying, and you are yelling."

"All right, Molly," he said. "You're a big girl now. Let's talk. Put supper aside for now, Ruth, until this is finished."

Motioning us all to the table, Father looked at me gravely, and then lowered his eyes. We sat in silence for what seemed like a lifetime.

"Molly, you know about the financial crisis. I guess I should have shared more openly about what has been happening."

I nodded in cautious agreement.

"I didn't want to worry you without reason. I hoped we would be spared the problems so many people have been experiencing recently, but—it is not to be."

Mama reached out for Father's hand. "Things will work out, Hank," she said. "They always have in the past."

I could not imagine what was coming. I waited in anticipation, without even drawing a breath. What was Father about to say?

"Molly, I was given notice earlier this week that my company is closing, going out of business."

Okay. People lose jobs. I understood. I waited for more.

"I hate to tell you this, but it seems if we're going to continue to live and eat, I need to take work in Chicago. I have checked out various possibilities, and this seems the best fit."

"Do you see now, Molly?" Mama asked in her soft-spoken voice.

"We will make out all right, Father, and if you have to work in the city, I understand."

"Thanks for your help, Molly. I know it will not be easy on any of us. We will need to move in a little more than a month. Right before Christmas," Father said with a grimace.

"Pardon me?" I said. It was like I was awakened from my slumber. I waited for him to repeat himself because I must have misunderstood. Father offered no eye contact. I thought he meant he would come home on the weekends. There was a train route straight from Royal Oak to Chicago so that would work. I finally spoke up to fill the silence.

"Did you say we're … we're moving … in December? To Chicago with Al Capone and the rest of the gangsters?" I said elevating my voice, now dripping with sarcasm.

"We can't keep our home, Molly. I can't pay for it. But I can hire out to the failed businesses in Chicago to help close their financial records. There are many companies shutting down. That might pay our bills for a little while anyway," he explained.

I stood up, feeling sick, and dashed down the hall to the bathroom. Everything I knew and loved in the only town I'd ever known washed over my consciousness. I made it to the commode and heaved. No relief. I was queasy, but empty. Father could not have meant what he said. I must have misunderstood.

There had to be another way to handle this. Surely Father hadn't looked hard enough in Detroit. He only learned he needed a new job this week. There had to be some other employment possibilities. It was evident that Father wasn't thinking of me when he made this mammoth, independent decision. Then again, that would not be unusual.

I would not go. I simply would not. I would find a way to stay in Royal Oak. Maybe I could move in with Winnie. Yes, they would take me. I knew they would.

Feeling lightheaded, I slid to the floor.

"Molly, Molly? Dear, are you all right? Can I help you?" Mama called through the door.

After regaining my composure, I stood up and opened the door. I looked into Mama's troubled face, but stormed on past her. Father was standing in front of the window, staring into the black of night.

"I'm sorry, Father, but I cannot move with you," I announced with all the determination a young girl could muster. I had never ever in my entire life talked back to Mama or Father.

"Molly, you will come with us," Father countered. "Trust me."

"I will not move to Chicago," I declared with more volume and fierce conviction.

"You are our daughter and you will move with us. Next month, we will not even own this house. The bank will. Plain and simple," Father said.

Force met force.

"You just don't understand, do you? No! You really do not," I said even louder. By then, I was crying. Carry Nation fighting for prohibition couldn't have been more authentic.

"Molly, it is you, not me. You do not understand. I have no choice," he fired back.

"Father, there must be another choice. How could you

have concluded this is the only option? I have the concert in January, my high school, all my friends, the only home I've ever known, and you expect me to move to Chicago during my senior year?" Exasperation dripped from every syllable.

Father's iron gaze permeated the room. My stinging words hung thick in the air. I knew I had crossed the line. He reached towards me. If I'd been younger, he probably would have swatted my backside. I pulled away. Glancing at Mama out of the corner of my eye, I could see her distress. Caught in the middle, she didn't know whether to hug me or send me to my room.

"Molly, I'll do everything possible to get you back for the concert," Father said in a gravelly, unsteady voice.

"And you think that will fix everything?" I shouted. At that, I bolted from the dining room.

"You never have understood me!" I hollered back, slamming my bedroom door behind me.

As I locked the door, the darkness in my room barely hinted at the depths of my despair. It was the perfect setting for my demolished dreams. Heaving myself across my bed, my tears flowed without restraint. I had never experienced such rage and grief.

Dear God, HELP ME! I know I have hurt my parents. Please forgive me, but ...

I looked out my window. A sliver of new moon rimmed with moisture crystals hung suspended in the universe. A glimmer of light in the black velvet sky. Perhaps it promised a shred of hope, a glimpse of God's mercy.

I know you are there, God, somewhere. Please don't hide from me now.

Chapter 11—There Must Be a Way

My head. Ohhhh. Did a torpedo hit me in the night? My heart—such emptiness. Hearing Mama rustle in the kitchen, I glanced at my clock. I rolled out of bed ever so slowly with aches in parts of my body I never knew were there. I raked through my hair as Father's news seeped into my consciousness.

Today was the day I'd been looking forward to for months, the live rehearsal. I paused at the mirror, seeing ugly, swollen red eyes. Dark circles hung like raccoon masks from my restless, tearful night. I splashed cold water on my face and held the wash cloth to my eyes, hoping to heal the damage. Glamour would be out of the question for this rehearsal.

Maybe this would be the only chance I'd have to play with the orchestra. Maybe I would not even be here in January. I slammed my hands down on the bathroom sink, mad at myself for being such a mess. Mad at the world for making such a mess.

I will play with the symphony in January. Why would I have won the audition if I were not supposed to play? Isn't that why you allowed this opportunity to come into my life, God? So, I could fulfill the purpose you have for me?

I decided to go with the old saying that all would work out for the best. After all, I prayed last night. I would continue praying until God answered. Shrugging at my course of action, I dressed. Nothing too fancy today. I pulled on a royal blue skirt and paired it with a plain white blouse. Comfortable enough. My directions were to come casual since this was a rehearsal.

At breakfast, Mama and I pretended nothing had happened. Of course. Emotions were tucked away. How we performed these scenes of denial was cause for amazement. Maybe my parents and I could go to Hollywood and make some money for our unbelievable acting.

Mama knew better than to mention my rebellious words before the rehearsal. I didn't want to talk about any of it. She wrapped a couple of peanut butter sandwiches and apple slices in waxed paper and slid them into her large purse.

Father drove us to the station, resulting in a solemn ride. In all honesty, I was relieved. I didn't want to talk about my emotional outburst or the move to Chicago. As Mama and I rode the train into the city once again, I remembered the excitement of my audition trip. What a difference a few weeks made. I curled up in my seat with eyes closed, signaling I was not open for business as usual. Mama read.

About ten o'clock, we entered Orchestra Hall and walked the lengthy aisle of the auditorium. The strings were warming up on stage. Each musician was practicing independently, producing quite the discord. The brass instruments announced their timbre, and the percussion players rolled and tapped with no coherent rhythm. My head pounded with lingering effects from the previous night while the cacophony compounded its misery. As I approached the stage, the conductor motioned for me to come up. He halted the musicians' warmup, and pointed to the first chair oboe to provide the "A" note for tuning. The concertmaster drew his bow across the "A" for all the strings to match.

I climbed the steps and walked behind that same heavy curtain as when I auditioned. I walked more confidently and without hesitation, parted the weighty velvet separating me from the orchestra. On center stage, the glimmering black Steinway was placed in front of the musicians, but off to the left of the conductor. After adjusting the stool for my size, I scanned the musicians with their eyes now beaded on me. I decided I had sure proof my heart was still in me because it raced with fury.

"Miss Martin, I would like to introduce you to our superb symphony orchestra members," said the conductor. "I am Maestro Walsh, and I welcome you to this distinctive group of musicians."

I smiled and acknowledged his introduction, hoping no one would notice the peculiar puffiness under my eyes. If only I wore glasses to help disguise the swelling.

"I would like for you to meet Miss Molly Martin, the outstanding student artist from Royal Oak High School who earned the privilege of performing," he added.

At that, the string players tapped their bows on the music stands, and other musicians clapped. I felt small—young and insignificant before these professionals. Yet I was honored to receive their approval. I smiled and stood, acknowledging their kind applause before reseating myself.

"Miss Martin, please prepare yourself for the concerto," the conductor announced.

Now came the test of my life. I spoke a quick silent prayer. God, please forgive my anger and frustration. Please give me a mind that can think clearly, and hands that can play their best.

I paused for a deep breath with my hands poised above the keys. Stroking each introductory bass chord with first intentional, and then, thunderous determination, I felt energy rising within me. The strings began the haunting melody with my accompaniment of finger runs up and down octaves. My hands and brain both happily responded to the hours, days, weeks, and months of practice. The beauty of the music once again embraced every inch of me—mind, body, and soul. We continued through the concerto almost flawlessly. I felt beads of perspiration form on my brow, yet it seemed we were an experienced team. Hand and glove.

I was weary and perspiring, but persisted through to the dramatic ending. This time the orchestra applauded spontaneously. I stood up smiling with relief, and the conductor stepped off the podium to give me a congratulatory hug. I could only think how grateful I was for God's gift. I knew without doubt, this was, indeed, his calling on my life.

"Take a fifteen-minute break, and we will rehearse some individual passages," Maestro Walsh announced. "Good work, everyone."

We were finished by lunchtime. Mama and I thanked everyone and began the short journey home. Walking to the station, I listened to Mama's heels clicking on the sidewalk and remembered all the fun we once had together. Little lunch trips to the city, window shopping, and sometimes buying clothes and shoes. Now, in a wink of an eye, we were among the poor. For sure, there was no money for shopping or celebratory lunches at a restaurant. In fact, Mama said there was no money for anything. I suddenly remembered how Father said the symphony might not have patrons who can afford tickets. Or, the symphony might not have money to pay the musicians. The somber talk of the night before smacked my happy memories into submission.

"Molly, I'm extremely proud of you. Your performance was beautiful. You seemed at ease even though this was your first time with the symphony. How did it feel?" Mama asked.

"I was tired, and my mind was distracted, but then when the music began …"

I stopped and looked into Mama's eyes.

"You do know, Mama. I must be here for this concert. It's all I've ever dreamed about. There must be another way than moving to Chicago."

"Molly, please know that your father and I will do all that we can to help. We do understand. However, you must think of what your father is going through too."

In my mind, I knew my defense. Father is not losing a lifetime dream. He's losing a job. I didn't dare say a word.

On the way home, I rode in purposeful isolation, picking at the peanut butter sandwich Mama had packed. At last, I rested my head on the window ledge. Negative thoughts, go away. Between the pounding of my headache and the rhythmic clacking of the train wheels, I finally dozed off.

"Molly, we're almost home," Mama said, gently touching my shoulder.

"Oh. Oh, we're home?" I asked, stretching my arms from my curled-up position.

"Royal Oak, Woodward Station." I heard the conductor announce as he strolled through the cars.

The rhythmic clacking of the wheels on the tracks slowed and the long whistle declared our arrival. I saw Father waving from below. His face bore a kind expression, so that was good. I wanted to share my success, but after my insolence Friday, maybe it would be best to let him take the lead. I had no idea how Father would feel.

"Hello to my two favorite girls," Father quipped as we climbed down the steps.

Mama gave him a warm hug and kiss on the cheek. I gave a polite smile.

"How did everything go, Molly?" he inquired, looking me in the eye.

"Very well, Father."

I felt so awkward. Between our two smiling faces stood an ocean of untold emotions. If someone had taken a photograph of us at that moment, I wondered what the caption would have been.

"Oh, Hank, it was exceptional. Everyone said so. The conductor was kind, and the orchestra members were positively receptive. You really will enjoy the concert in January."

Mama took Father's hand as we all walked to the car.

"That is good news, Molly," Father said, looking in my direction. "You are a very hardworking, talented young lady. I commend you."

"Thank you," I replied, thankful for Father's kind words.

My heart flooded with competing emotions—joy, fear, sadness, remorse, worry. No words for small talk seemed appropriate. Saying thank you would have to do. We still had the most incomprehensible challenge before us.

Father drove. Mama bantered about the leftovers she would fix for dinner. I watched my beloved hometown slip by like colorful pieces in a kaleidoscope. My hometown. My heart. I could not move away.

Chapter 12—My Red Sea

Considering my disrespectful actions Friday night, I was shocked that Father could even pretend he was proud of me yesterday. I had never ever said, "No" to his requests or demands. I had never ever walked away from him, ignoring his declarations. I was confident Mama would love me no matter what. But Father? This was way different from any childhood insurrection. Would he be relieved when I was out on my own?

Our old Packard automobile shook and whined as Father tried starting it that grey Sunday morning. After some cajoling, the car shook into forward motion by jerks and starts. It must have felt like us. We, too, were trying with great effort and groanings, to move forward. Yet our disturbing ugliness was in plain sight. The crisp November weather didn't come close to the unreconciled chill inside our car. Despite efforts to restore normalcy, we knew relationships were bruised and battered. Mama would never hold grudges even when she was upset. Father put on his best, stoic, good father response to my good news yesterday. I knew I had some work to do. Forgiveness was not coming quickly.

I wrapped my arms around myself, bracing against the cold air as we rode to church. Maybe I should try singing to shatter the silence. Maybe not. Mama and Father would think I had lost my mind. Scrunching up in the backseat,

I pulled my red, wrap over coat to cover my silk stockings. They might appear stylish, but they were not practical.

As we filed into the sanctuary, I wasn't looking around for peers as in the past. We marched down the aisle and took our seats near the front as usual. All I could think about was my father had no job. Our home was not ours. My parents were moving to Chicago. I was staying in Royal Oak. But I didn't know how.

After several hymns, everyone turned for the morning greeting. I plastered on a faint smile, feeling as displaced as a beached fish.

"Good morning, Mrs. West. Yes, I am fine. And, how are you and the family?"

"Oh, hello, Mr. Thompson. It is good to see you too."

What a relief when I was free to sit and simmer in my own lousy thoughts.

After morning announcements, Pastor McDonald began. I knew I should listen. You have my attention, God. You really do. I don't have any answers.

Most of the sermon was about victorious people from the Bible. Young David won his battle with the giant Goliath. Joshua took over the city of Jericho, but only because he obeyed God's directions. Then, of course, there was Moses who took the people across the Red Sea. I knew all of this. Mama read those stories to me when I was little. As we left the morning service, I shrugged. What were you saying, Lord? What about my Red Sea, my Jericho, my Goliath?

After lunch, Mama picked up her knitting and went into the living room. She always made us new sweaters for winter so she had projects. Mama noticed me going toward my room with the library book, The Trumpeter of Krakow.

"What are you reading? You don't often read for pleasure," Mama said.

"The librarian recommended it. We have to read for English, you know. It's a Newbery winner from last year. Hope it's good."

Father was engrossed in the depressing newspaper, lost in his world of business. The house became so still it seemed vacant. I wondered what would become of it when we left. After supper, I called Winnie. I wanted to talk to Jack so much, but Mama said young ladies should never pursue. What agony to wait for Jack to initiate. C'mon, Jack. Be bold.

I hoped the operator wasn't Mrs. Burr, the busybody. I was grateful the line wasn't tied up on a Sunday afternoon when everybody seemed to call friends and family.

"Hello, Mama March. How are you doing?" I said, trying to rally some good cheer.

"Oh, we're fine. How was your rehearsal? We were rooting for you, you know."

"It was thrilling. Thanks for asking. I'm so excited about the upcoming concert."

"Wonderful. We hope to be there. Let me call Winnie, and please give your parents my regards."

"Winnifred—phone call."

"How was it, Molly? Tell me."

"The rehearsal was marvelous. In fact, that's the reason I'm calling," I said. "But I do still have an enormous problem. No joke."

"I don't understand. First, a marvelous rehearsal, and now a problem?"

"Winnie, I must play this concerto with the symphony."

"Of course." Winnie's voice sounded perplexed, nearly impatient because she didn't understand.

"Winnie, my father has lost his job."

"Ohhhh, no. I'm so sorry."

"I didn't know until Friday evening. My parents are moving to Chicago."

"Chicago?"

"We have to be out of our home before Christmas"

Suddenly, I heard a click-click on the phone line.

"Oh, no," I whispered.

After a long pause, Winnie asked, "Molly? Are you still on?"

"Yes, but I think we should talk tomorrow. Someone is listening. Can you meet me after school?"

"Sure. Fine. See you at the lockers."

Click, and I was off, with the phone's earpiece dangling in my hand. In my haste to share, I had revealed my family's business. "Mrs. Nosey" could easily compound my problem, and now everyone would know by the day's end. I sat speechless. And, ashamed. How could I have been so careless?

After school the next day, Jack spotted us when Winnie and I were about to leave.

"Hey, Molly and Winnie," he called. "Are you on your way home now?"

"We're going to the soda shop, Jack. Want to come?" I said.

Wearing his bright smile, Jack reached for my hand.

He squeezed his fingers around mine in a most comforting way.

"Jack, I have a huge problem." I looked into his eyes, wishing so much that he could fix my woes.

"What's wrong, Molly?" Jack asked, staring back with curiosity.

I began retelling my story: the news of our move, Father yelling, and how sick I felt.

"And the worst part of all is … I said I would not move."

Jack grimaced. His eyes softened as he searched my eyes to understand.

"Maybe you could stay with us, Molly," Winnie said. "You know my parents love you like a daughter."

"I don't know if my parents will let me, even if yours will. They believe, since I'm their daughter, I must go with them. You know. 'A family should stay together.' Under normal circumstances, I would agree."

"Could you come back in the summer?" Jack asked.

"That's more likely. But, Jack, I must play with the symphony in January. It's my sole opportunity to make a name for myself as an upcoming pianist."

"There must be a way," Jack said.

"We'll figure something out," Winnie added.

With trust in Jack and Winnie's responses, my confidence lifted, maybe one tiny notch. A memory verse popped into my mind as we sat down to order sodas.

"A Scripture just came to me," I said after we ordered. "Do you remember where it says God's unfailing love is new every morning? I think it was King David talking. He goes on to say how he trusted in God. What do you think that means?

"I'm not a Bible teacher," Winnie laughed. "Maybe a chemistry whiz, but not a biblical scholar. Where is the verse?"

"Somewhere in Psalms. I think it was King David writing. But if I want something with all my heart, can I trust God to make it happen?' I asked.

"Hmmmm. What if God has a better idea? Something better than you ever imagined?" Jack asked.

I looked down and swished the straw around in my Coca-Cola. After a minute or so, I looked up to see my two best friends staring at me.

"I think I will have to pray about that."

When I went to bed that night, I was still wrestling with the idea that God had a better idea. I knew he was all-knowing. Yet, my heart did not want to let go of my dreams. Didn't God give me those dreams? And the talent?

Mama taught me the twenty-third Psalm when I was very young. I will never forget the first line. "The Lord is my Shepherd; I shall not want." Was this true? If so, then I should have this gift you have given me. I want to trust you, God, yet I feel as powerless as a pea in Mama's garden, waiting to be plucked. Help me in my unbelief.

Chapter 13—Not the Piano!

"Hello, World, I am Molly. I was once an outstanding pianist with a promising future. Now I am a pitiful girl moving to Chicago against my will."

I used to talk to myself as a form of entertainment when I was growing up. After all, I was an only child. Today, I found nothing humorous about my spoken declarations. Instead, I inwardly screamed no, no, no! How could they do this? How could they have hidden this from me?

Mama kept reminding me how things could be worse. I tried pretending I was once a very wealthy person and lost my fortune. It didn't help a bit. I had never experienced wealth, so how could I know such loss? Was it too much to ask God to give me my own everyday life back? Maybe it was an ordinary life, a little bit dull even, but it held the promise of a bright future doing something I was passionate about.

Father said moving to Chicago beat standing in bread lines waiting on handouts to fill my belly. I soberly acknowledged his truth.

President Hoover called for us to band together and help one another during this precarious time. He made it sound so short term. Even if it were a short season of loss, in my estimation some losses were not recoverable.

November crawled by in a blur of disappointment, riddled by my inept attempts at being an overcomer. Yet,

Thanksgiving had to happen. We were duty-bound to give thanks. How could we not? We had food and a warm place to sleep. However, Thanksgiving 1929 was different.

Mama roasted a puny little chicken, but it was a chicken, at least. I giggled as I pulled the oven door open to check on the roasting hen.

"Mama, I think that is the tiniest chicken I've ever seen."

"I know, Molly, but we have to be grateful we have even one small chicken this year."

"Yes, yes, I know, Mama. Father has made that abundantly clear. You do know I'm thankful for our food, don't you?"

As a tradition, we drove out to the countryside to find a tom turkey for our annual Thanksgiving meal. There was one local farmer we visited every year. November, 1929, our turkey farmer was nowhere around. I wondered what his fate had been. The old farmhouse was deserted, and nary a turkey could be found gobbling.

"I am so thankful for a good harvest from our garden so I could put some of our vegetables away for winter. Here, Molly, would you please make the dough balls for our dinner rolls? Thank you," Mama said, using a happy sing-song voice.

I sang my answer back, just to be silly. "Roll, roll, roll the dough, gently as we go."

Mama laughed. I had so many fond memories of the two of us working together in the kitchen. It was easy to reminisce about those happier times. Mama did her best to be pennywise with any spending, even on our so-called Thanksgiving feast. For what the pitiful chicken was missing in meaty goodness, Mama compensated with other delicious side dishes. We could fill up on homegrown green beans and corn without a problem.

Mama's garden, which was the pride of her summer work, took up most of our small backyard. The corn always stood so tall that it created a natural privacy fence between our yard and the neighbor behind.

When all the food was ready, we gathered around the same table where we had enjoyed happy days, and more recently, some very tumultuous days.

"Molly, you begin," Father said as we settled at the table. "Think of two things you're grateful for."

I paused to reflect on the past couple of months and how life had changed in such a dramatic way. I spoke without looking up from my place. Sometimes, no eye contact was best.

"I am grateful for God's provision in many ways, including our food and warm shelter. I am thankful he allowed me the chance to play once with the symphony. I am most grateful he is allowing me to begin a career as a musician." I looked back up to see the reaction.

"And, you, Ruth?" Father asked, shifting from the now-exposed "elephant in the room"—the move, the piano, my dream.

"I am thankful for the two of you, the most important people in my life. I am thankful that we have food to keep us healthy," she answered.

Father concluded with a smile. "I am thankful for a way to provide for us. I am grateful for both my beautiful wife, and my talented daughter."

He turned and looked me in the eyes. I could feel his affection, despite all we had been through. I tried to receive it as sincere—from his heart. Yet, Father could not resist another tiny lecture about how well off we were, on top of all his other sermons. I guess he felt he had to reinforce his intended outcome, grateful hearts without complaint. Yes, sir!

Mama's best light and fluffy yeast rolls were the final touch of goodness to fill us that day. We didn't have enough sugar to bake a pie this year, but we were all stuffed without any sweets. Even I could appreciate all our blessings.

One early December afternoon, I saw Jack talking with his friend Jerry at school. As I approached, I overheard some, but I had no idea what was wrong. Illness? Death? Money? "Honestly, I am so sorry about your uncle, Jerry," Jack said. He motioned me to step closer. "Hi, sweetheart," he said with a bare hint of a smile.

Oh, how my heart stirred when he called me 'sweetheart.' He had never used that term of endearment before. But, why the mournful face?

"Molly, I'm sure you've heard of some of the very wealthiest people who have lost their entire fortunes. Many are not coping with this," Jack said. Then, he looked back at Jerry whose eyes were somber, as if reliving someone's grief. I didn't think it proper to ask any specifics. I didn't know Jerry very well, and he probably wouldn't want me to know his personal business.

"Oh, yes," I said. "My Father makes sure I understand we are not the only ones having to make sacrifices. He reads some of those sad articles from the newspaper to us every evening just so we know how bad it is," I added. I was almost chuckling as I thought of Father's routine.

Jack and Jerry lightened up. I guess they were also

amused at my rendition of Father's ways.

"Imagine once being truly rich, and ending up begging for food," I said.

On my walk home, I pondered all the suicides being caused by great financial losses. It was the once-wealthy people who had been jumping from the top of buildings. Did they feel they couldn't live without their comforts? The thought of ending my life because I was poor, or even hungry, was beyond my comprehension. However, I had never been blessed with riches. So much hopelessness and despair embraced our nation.

While many Americans still clung to the hope, or wish, that things would get better, I also put one foot in front of another to persevere in school. In all honesty, none of it seemed to matter anymore, if it ever did. Not that I'd ever invested my energies in school, but I didn't want to fail. I plodded through one slow and boring day at a time, thankful that Mama and Father had not seen my grades. I knew someday soon, very soon, the truth would come out, but maybe they wouldn't care by then.

Mr. Hill didn't bother me much these days. Perhaps he had given up on me too. I didn't know if he was depressed, or whether he stopped believing I had potential. Overall, the spirit at Royal Oak High School was diminished, quieter, more serious. Even the rah-rah sports enthusiasts lost their school spirit.

Mr. Clancy continued to give me piano lessons though we couldn't afford to pay. I wondered how he and his wife paid their bills, but, of course, it was not appropriate to ask. For me, piano lessons were the best part of each week, keeping me prepared and somewhat encouraged. Together, we studied the Beethoven Sonata Pathétique, a few Bach

Etudes, and some lighthearted Chopin waltzes to round things off. Of course, I had to continue fine-tuning the concerto. Perfection could never be left to chance, and the January concert was only a few weeks away.

I shuffled up the back porch steps in my snowy boots, stomping twice to clean them. Mama peered out of the kitchen window. Pulling my galoshes off, I set them on the mat inside to dry. A sweet scent wafted in my direction.

"Sugar?" I asked. Mama hadn't baked sweets since Father lost his job. "Mmmmm. Something sure smells good in here."

"Would you like to help decorate some cookies? I saved some sugar, so we could celebrate."

"What, Mama? Celebrate what? Did Father find a job?"

"No, dear. No. However, we are about to celebrate Christmas, aren't we?"

Soon Christmas would be upon us, though it would be different this year. Christmas would be unlike all the others I had ever known. The idea of gift giving seemed more of a nagging reminder than an expected celebration. So many people were out of work. Even so, I looked forward to a break from school. Only one more week.

"I'd love to have a cookie with you, Mama, even though I'd rather Father had a job. Here. In Royal Oak. Or even Detroit."

"I wish so too, dear. Let's pray about that right now." Mama reached for my hands. "Dear Father God, we really love you and need you. Please help us find your will for us in this difficult time. Thank you. Amen."

Mama reassured me with her sweet smile. God would take care of everything.

"Thank you," I said remembering all the times Mama had quoted the twenty-third Psalm when I was young.

Lightening her tone, she went on. "Now, let's celebrate with some music and cookies."

The warmth and security of being together in our home brought me a sense of peace I hadn't felt for weeks. It felt like the life I had loved and the security I once knew.

"Play some Christmas carols for us, and we can sing for a bit," Mama said. She finished stirring our chicken noodle soup and popping biscuits in the oven. "Okay now. What should we sing while we wait for Father and the biscuits? Won't he be surprised when he walks in?"

It was already dark outside, so Father was expected soon. Moments later, we heard his snowy boots stomping on the steps. We continued singing with great gusto: "Hark! The Herald Angels Sing ..."

Father hung up his coat, and walked into the living room with a seldom seen smile.

"What a surprise we have here," he remarked. After listening for a minute, he finished the refrain with us: "With th' angelic host proclaim, Christ is born in Bethlehem. Hark! the herald angels sing, Glory to the new-born King!"

"What smells so delicious? Must be something besides our quite familiar chicken soup," Father commented, as we gathered at the table.

"Cookies, cookies," Mama and I answered almost in unison.

"It seems like forever since we've had dessert," he added with a wink. "Where did you find sugar?"

"I squirreled away my pantry stash when you lost your

job, Hank. I knew there would be an occasion when we would want something special."

"You're a wise woman, Ruth. And so practical. Speaking of our finances," Father said, "I found out today our move-out date will be December 20. I know this is not the best timing, but at least we'll have some days to get settled before Christmas."

"Hank, can we please save this conversation until after supper?"

I dug in, unwilling to postpone details about our move.

"Have you seen the size of our apartment yet, Father?"

I imagined my piano squished into one end of a tiny living room, even smaller than ours.

"Yes, Molly, when I went to Chicago last week, I was able to take a tour. I think I mentioned it's not too far from Lake Michigan. Should be fun for you in the summer."

"I'm thinking more about January, right now, Father."

Mama gave me one of her STOP NOW looks. I thought how much I'd rather be at Orchard Lake swimming with Winnie and my friends from Royal Oak. I could see myself sitting alone on the beach with a hoard of strangers.

"Let's clear off the table and do some planning," Father said.

We all helped clean up before resuming our conversation in the dining room. I could remember too clearly the last family talk we had after Father lost his job. This time, Mama passed around the cookie tray as if we were having a celebration.

"Gee, Father, I have so many questions churning in my head. How are we getting all our stuff to Chicago? What does the apartment look like? How far away is my school?"

"Slow down, Molly." Father chuckled. "One thing at a time. First, our place is on the third floor. The building is five stories high. Our apartment is small, but one advantage is the heat will rise from the lower floors. We will be cozy during the winter, for sure."

"Hank, I hadn't even thought about that. It will be a help in January and February." After a pause, Mama added, "Hmmm, but I wonder how hot it will be next summer."

"The apartment is on the end of the floor, so that will also help keep it quieter," Father went on, ignoring Mama's rhetorical question.

"That's good too because when I practice, only one adjoining apartment will hear me."

Father proceeded, avoiding my comment as well.

"Mr. Thomas will move what fits in his truck and what fits in our apartment."

Slowly casting his eyes downward, Father's words shifted from casual to cautious.

"Do you remember meeting George when you stopped by work that day, Ruth?"

"I'm not sure I do, but I am thankful he's available to help."

"He said he could make two trips, if he must, but it will cost twice as much, of course."

"Father, how will we get the piano to the third floor?" I asked.

Father took a long drink of water. We waited expectantly. At least, I waited expectantly. Maybe Mama already knew.

"Well, Molly, the piano won't fit in George's truck," Father said. After even a longer pause, he added, "Or in the apartment."

Father avoided eye contact after dropping that goose egg.

"After things settle down, maybe we can get a smaller upright for you."

"After things 'settle down,' you say? Father! Do you really mean that you intend to leave my beautiful grand piano behind? You realize upright pianos don't have the same key touch, or the same tone quality. Don't you, Father? But, forget that. This is the one thing that really matters to me, and you have dismissed it with such ease?"

I looked at Mama, pleading for help. "Mama?"

"Well, Molly, this is the best I can do for us right now," Father said.

"So, I am supposed to just leave my life, the Music Conservatory, my dreams? I'm supposed to move in submission to your plans, leaving all the years I've spent becoming the best pianist I can be? Mama, do you really expect me to walk away from playing with the symphony, nodding glibly in compliance?

I stood up in disbelief at this latest disclosure.

"I suppose you have a wonderful person all picked out to take my grand piano off your hands," I added, straining to control my rage. "And when did you think I should learn of this, Father? The day of our move? You knew how small the apartment is. You rented it. You knew how small the truck is. You hired the man for heaven's sake. And, without a word of warning!"

I shoved my chair back to the table and ran down

the hallway to my room. The mahogany bedroom door slammed behind me creating a resounding exclamation—something that was never done in our home. Tonight was different. I didn't care if I was polite, or not. My real father would never have sold our piano. Never!

I heard Father raise his voice, his words trailing me down the hall. "What about our dreams and our lives, Molly? What about our losses? You are not the only one in this family!"

No wonder I remembered the last "family talk" with horror. This was a repeat of the appalling night when Father lost his job. And, to think Mama and I had just prayed together, and we had all sung Christmas carols together in sweet harmony. What is wrong with this family? Even as my head pounded like a sledge hammer, I could not stop my remembering—a sweet Thanksgiving followed by the worst tragedy ever. What else could happen?

Chapter 14—Life? Without Music?

Escape. That's all I wanted. I desperately wanted out of the house. I would have simply stayed in bed if I hadn't wanted to avoid Father and Mama so much. All day. Latin? Chemistry? History? Why should any of it matter? All that fretting about Mr. Hill and chemistry. For nothing. Even Mr. Hill's threat to cut my Conservatory privileges didn't matter now. I was moving to Chicago in a few days and probably wouldn't have the same classes. So what if I failed.

"Winnie!" I called, spying her in the distance. I dragged my feet down the hall toward my first class. Shoulder to shoulder with armfuls of books, I wormed my way through the students, all seemingly committed to avoiding a tardy. Of course, we were not supposed to run in the halls, but even making forward movement was difficult that morning.

"Excuse me. Excuse me," I repeated. I mouthed the polite words, but I really didn't care if anyone was upset as I bumped in and out of the crowd. I wanted to get Winnie's attention before I lost her. Winnie turned her head just in time to see me waving my free arm like a windmill. Smiling, she backed flush against the wall to let me catch up.

"Molly, it's good to see you," Winnie said in her usual friendly way.

"I don't know why I'm even at school today, but where else would I go?" I said, answering my own question with a shrug.

"Goodness gracious, Molly. Your eyes are swollen like you cried a river of tears."

"My life is upside down and backwards," I replied.

"That sounds melodramatic. Tell me what's wrong!"

I wrinkled my nose, and my mouth twisted as I tried to choke out an answer. I was such a mess. "I will try. Meet me at our lockers at lunch."

The teachers droned on in every class. It was so meaningless now. After what seemed like four days instead of four hours, the bell rang for lunch break. I saw Winnie waiting for me, but not wearing her usual happy face.

"Do you want to go across the street?" she asked.

Seeing the students streaming into the lunch area, I wanted out. Every inch of me wanted to run, hide, or even better, disappear. Forever. Then I remembered the assembly hall. It would be secluded. "Let's go sit in the auditorium where we can have some privacy, okay?"

"Tell me what's going on," Winnie said as she followed me toward the front of the school. "What could be so awful? I've never seen you act so, so … disturbed."

We cautiously approached the double doors that led into the darkened auditorium. Scanning the hall and entrance to the office for adults, I eased open the door and slipped inside with Winnie at my back.

"Glad for the fire escape signs for some light," I whispered. We fumbled our way to the first row and slid into some end seats.

"This is creepy. Shouldn't we find another place?" Winnie said. "What if someone saw us enter, or worse yet, Principal Hyde catches us? Are you sure you want to risk getting caught in here?"

The shadowy dark auditorium was in perfect alignment with my despair.

"Nobody will look for us here," I replied. "If you want your sandwich, go ahead and eat. I have no appetite."

"Sandwiches aren't important right now. What's going on, Molly? Why are you acting so strange?"

"My father told me about our move last night."

"But you already knew you were moving on Saturday."

"Winnie." My voice started choking up. The next words stuck somewhere between my brain and my lips.

Grabbing my arm, Winnie shook me. "What, Molly? What? Tell me!"

"Father is selling my piano," I said with trembling voice.

Most people could not grasp its significance, but I knew Winnie would. The consequences of such a loss could only matter to a musician like me, and those who knew her heart.

"What? Your piano?"

My tightly wrapped grief began to unravel as Winnie reached for my hand and gave it a light squeeze.

"I'm sorry, Winnie, but I must go."

I squeezed her hand back as a gentle thank you, and pulled away. Here I was again—trapped with no foreseeable way out, and with no control over any of it. Oh, how clever my spiritual enemy was throwing stinging darts from my broken past. He knew well that this time, Mama could not rescue me as she once did from the Children's Home.

"Where are you going?" Winnie pleaded, once again

following me.

My head was cast downward to avoid looks at my face, swollen eyes webbed with tears. I needed to leave. I could not pretend my way through the rest of the ordinary day.

"Do you want me to come with you? What can I do for you?" Winnie pleaded, while trailing me.

The bell rang, signaling the start of my next class, but I grabbed my coat and turned to hug Winnie goodbye.

"I'll be praying for you," Winnie whispered into my ear.

I nodded and headed for the exit. I was greeted with a blast of December Michigan air. How appropriately bitter. Where could I go? Not home. Not church.

I began pleading as my feet pounded faster and faster on the sidewalk.

"God, why are you letting this happen? I worked so hard. You gave me this talent. And now? You're supposed to be a loving God. How can this be?"

The more I argued with God, the faster I walked until my gait broke into a run. I was going nowhere.

Chapter 15—A Solemn Peace

My feet pounded the sidewalk. The sharp smack of my shoes against the solid ground permeated the frigid air. The walls of my chest were so tight, I could hardly breathe. I ran a few blocks before I slowed enough to catch my breath. It was then that it dawned on me. I was very near the Conservatory.

As I approached the building, I could see Mr. Clancy through the front windows. He appeared intrigued with a stack of music on one of the pianos. I started walking slowly toward the house. Should I interrupt him? No. I turned away. Then, in an instant more, I did an about face. First, my feet were on the stairs. Then my finger pressed the doorbell. Finally, my mind gave permission for my impulsive decision.

I heard some shuffling inside as Mr. Clancy slowly made his way to the door, obviously not expecting a student.

"Coming. Coming," he called.

"Molly, I thought you were in school," he said in surprise. "What's the matter, dear? Your eyes—is it from the cold? Oh, never mind all that. Come right in, child, out of the frosty air."

He led me into the studio while calling to Mrs. Clancy. His once-tall stature appeared rounded and bent as he shuffled along in his house slippers.

"Miriam, you remember Molly. Could you bring some tea to warm her on this winter day?"

"Of course, dear," she called into the music suite. She appeared in a moment to greet me.

"What a pleasant surprise to see you today, Molly," Mrs. Clancy said, extending her arms in a welcoming hug.

"Thank you, Mrs. Clancy," I said, blowing lightly into my cupped hands to warm my fingers.

"I have a pot of tea on the stove now. It keeps us warmer on these winter days too."

I glanced at his beautiful grand pianos. Remembering the times Mr. Clancy and I played together, I walked over and gently stroked the keys. I looked up to see Mr. Clancy studying me.

"Come join me on the settee, Molly. Mrs. Clancy will bring some tea in a few minutes."

I sat, grateful for the comfort of this favorite place and this kind old man standing before me. More than a teacher, more than a musician, Mr. Clancy was a cherished friend. I knew he cared about my life.

"So, Molly, what brought you here today? I can see you're upset."

Before I could answer, Mrs. Clancy delivered our tea. Tiny blue and yellow pansy faces danced around the edges of my cup, making me smile again. I felt comforted and loved.

Wondering how to begin, I said, "We're moving Saturday."

"Yes, Molly, your mother told me," he responded.

"My piano."

"Yes?"

Clearing my throat, I finally choked out the words. "Father is selling it."

"Oh, my dear! How difficult for you."

We silently sipped our tea, letting the troubled matter rest quietly between us.

"Perhaps your parents can buy another piano after you settle," he answered softly.

"There is no money for a piano right now. Father doesn't even have work there. He hopes to get some contract jobs with companies who are going out of business. He's an accountant, you know."

"Don't lose heart, Molly. Sometimes we can only get a glimpse into our futures. I'm sure that is for our own good. Then we can't worry about what we don't know," he said.

I nodded as I clasped the teacup in my hands, grateful for its soothing warmth. At last, I felt my body relax in the quietness of the moment.

Mr. Clancy gave me a gentle smile. "Did you ever read about your hero Sergei Rachmaninoff's troubles?"

"I know his first major piece, a Prelude, wasn't a big hit. Did he feel bad when people asked him to perform?"

"Yes, indeed, he was not terribly proud of it. But, you know, the Concerto in C Minor, which you're playing, was his next composition. He also struggled with depression several times. Sergei didn't see himself as the success others did."

"Beethoven also had his problems, didn't he?"

"Certainly. Imagine losing your sight while trying to compose. And, perform." Mr. Clancy added, "He was an overcomer."

After some casual conversation, I put my teacup down and thanked Mr. Clancy for his kindness.

"Before you go, would you like to play the concerto? It will be good practice and a sweet memory," Mr. Clancy said.

"Of course. It may be my last time to play for a very long time."

"Now, Molly, don't think the worst. God may surprise you with an answer to your prayers. Maybe something you can't even imagine."

We walked across the room to the twin grands, and in moments began playing in classical unity. The tremendous introductory chords built to a perfect crescendo, filling the studio with its rich intensity. Once more, Rachmaninoff's melancholy romance gave my heavy heart wings to soar. Thank you, Lord.

"What a beautiful escape, Mr. Clancy. Thank you. I will never forget all you have done for me."

"You know you can stop by anytime. You have a great talent, Molly. Keep your faith. Remember, God has good plans for you."

Mrs. Clancy came to the door, and they both gave me a hug. I began the walk home, pondering everything. My steps were slow and deliberate. I must face my situation head on.

Lord, I need to hear from You.

As I came closer to the house, I wondered if I had just heard God's answer through Mr. Clancy. Keep the faith. God has good plans. Did I dare believe it?

When I arrived home, Mama was busy packing. Grocery store fruit crates sat on one side of the living room filled with pictures, a few knickknacks, and some of Mama's books. An auctioneer would sell the rest of our possessions on Friday.

Father said he was trying to find a buyer for the piano since it was more valuable, and we had so little money. If he couldn't, then it, too, would be auctioned for whatever price it would bring. He had posted the sale of it in the newspaper and had contacted schools and colleges as possible buyers. I wanted to be somewhere else if it went to auction. Watching my piano go to auction would be like selling a beloved pet to the lowest bidder. Heart wrenching.

"Molly, I was worried sick about you," Mama exclaimed as I removed my coat and gloves. I saw a flash of anger on her face.

"Why, Mama?" acting as if nothing could be wrong.

"I received a call this afternoon. You're lucky the truant officer didn't pick you up," she scolded.

"I had to get away. I talked to Winnie at lunch and my problems spilled over in tears. I couldn't go back to class like nothing was wrong."

"So, where have you been?" she asked with a bite in her tone.

"I walked. A long time. Ran a little too."

"In this cold? In school shoes?" Mama fussed in disbelief.

"Well, I ended up at Mr. Clancy's. Mrs. Clancy fixed tea, and we talked."

"Did you assume the school wouldn't call? After all, you skipped classes," she continued, sounding even more irritated.

"Mama, do I have to go back to school? We don't even know if my classes will be the same in Chicago. I'd rather just stay in my room and pack."

"You could pack in the evenings, you know. After all, you can only take a few boxes to our new apartment. We have explained that, Molly."

"I need to go lay down. I didn't sleep well last night."

Suppertime came without fanfare. Or conversation. I retreated to my room as soon as I could. Mama relented and decided to let me stay home Tuesday, Wednesday, and Thursday, and I was relieved. No more pretending my way through the normal class schedule.

I went through my chest of drawers, closet, and small desk. Winnie's mother called and talked with Mama for a while, but I didn't learn anything of their conversation. I'm sure Mrs. Nosey knew everything that was going on in our family by now. I stayed in my room with the door closed most of the week, and slept a lot.

Father knocked on my door. "Molly, phone for you," he said, without identifying the caller. I didn't answer immediately, so he went on. "Did you hear me, Molly? Phone call."

"Okay, Father," I answered, wondering who it could be. Everyone knew I was moving. I hoped it wasn't Jack. I couldn't bear telling him goodbye.

"This is Molly," I said with uncertainty.

"Hi," Winnie said. "It's me. I just had to let you know how worried Jack has been about you."

"Oh, it's good to hear from you. I didn't want to talk

to Jack yet. He's called here too. I asked Mama to tell him I wasn't feeling well because I didn't want to talk yet. I do plan to write him a letter tonight."

"A letter?" she queried.

"Yes, something he can read and reread," I replied. "I may not ever see Jack again, so I should go to school tomorrow. You know. Last goodbyes."

Suddenly, out of the blue, I burst out laughing. It sounded strange, even to me, after feeling so morose. It was the first laugh I had had for a whole week.

"What's so funny?" Winnie asked with a lilt in her voice. "Now that's the Molly I know and love."

"Honestly, after I said I would have my last goodbyes, I thought of Mr. Hill. Such a funny scene it would be! Do you suppose he will give me a goodbye hug?"

Then, I doubled over laughing. Instead of tears, hilarious laughter overcame both of us, unleashing a reservoir of emotion. Before we hung up, we laughed, then cried, and laughed even more. Such a marvelous catharsis.

Searching through my carefully packed box of writing paper and mementos, I noticed an old birthday card I'd saved. The lilac flower on the cover begged me to pick it up. Oh, the hope of springtime. I remember how happy I'd been just last April. So many good things were happening then. Sliding my finger between the front and inside page, I opened to see Mama's handwriting. Another expression of her forever love. On the left side of the page, she'd written a Scripture: "Be careful for nothing; but in everything by prayer and supplication with thanksgiving let your requests be made known unto God. And the peace of God, which passeth all understanding, shall keep your hearts and minds through Christ Jesus" (Philippians 4:6–7 KJV).

My tears began again. Stop, tears, STOP! I can't keep doing this. Oh, God. I do want your peace. You know my heart's cry.

I fell to my knees next to my bed. I knew my behavior had been despicable. I felt like a pouting child. I was a pouting child. I hated everything about my life.

Lord, please forgive me for my ungrateful heart. Fill me with your peace, God, and guard my selfish mind and heart.

After praying awhile, I stood up feeling a bit more determined. I could live through this. And, I could go to school tomorrow. I could tell my friends and teachers goodbye. At least my life in Royal Oak would end well.

I carefully put Mama's card back into my box and picked up a piece of writing paper. I began composing my thoughts to Jack. I used the special Parker fountain pen Father had given me for Christmas last year. They could be quite messy so I used extra care. No embarrassing ink spills on this letter would do, or tear stains either for that matter.

> Dear Jack,
>
> I'm sorry that I haven't been able to talk to you about what has been going on. I've had a hard time thinking anything positive about something that seems like a total loss. I don't want to leave Royal Oak. I thought I could work something out, like staying with Winnie's family. For now, at least, it seems there is no open door or way to escape this move. Winnie's family has not offered for me to board with them. We have no money to

pay anyone, and Mama would be heartbroken if I tried to do this on my own. You know, outright rebellion? Besides, how could I accomplish my dreams that way? Father has made his expectations clear.

You have been a wonderful friend and encourager. You listened to me share everything that has been good in my life. You always seemed to care about what is most important to me. Maybe I can spend some time with Winnie's family next summer, and we can all get together then. I hope we can stay in touch, and that I will see you again. You mean the world to me.

In fond friendship,

Molly

Chapter 16—Chicago, Chicago

Would Jack stay in touch after I left? Or would he find another someone to call his sweetheart? Would I ever see him again? Everything that I held dear was in a stage of flux. I slid my letter to Jack into the air vent of his locker Friday morning, just like always. At least, he would know my heart—well almost know my heart. I wanted to sign "With love" but decided I should wait for Jack to offer his love first as I had been taught.

Morning classes dragged by while I fought back tears. Graduating was one thing. This was another. During lunch, I didn't really sit down to eat. I had some hugs and well wishes from classmates with whom I had grown up from earliest school days. None of it seemed real. My goodbye to dear Mr. Hill was brief and unemotional. He acted nonchalant. He wouldn't have to worry with me, and he was no longer a thorn in my side. A victory for both of us. I was stoic. Even the dismissal bell announcing my last class, did not permeate my fog. Somehow my feet found their way to my locker, and I stared at it This was it. The end.

Pretending was over. For someone who wanted to be finished with school with all of her being, it seemed odd to feel even a twinge of sadness. I had already turned in my books, so it was time to clear out my locker. Pulling out a few loose papers jammed into the crevices, I studied them one by one. A little of this and a little of that, none of which was important enough to find its way home. An old algebra quiz. Not too awful. I crinkled up the page in a tight wad and tossed it into the nearby wastebasket. English, pretty good, overall. Chemistry—squash. Crinkle. Symbolically destroy.

"Good shot," Jack said laughing. I hadn't seen him approach from behind.

"Oh, hi," I said, smiling with uncertainty. I looked up into his face, recognizing again what a handsome young man he was. As well as kind and thoughtful. To think how he had showered his affection on me was humbling.

"It's good to see you," he replied, this time in a more serious tone. He dropped his eyes for a second, and after a pause, he went on. "I read your letter at lunch."

"I'm sorry I didn't return your call."

"I can only imagine how hard all of this has been."

I looked towards my locker, inwardly demanding my eyes not to weep.

"Well, I'd better finish up here, Jack. The auction …" My voice broke. I tried to stifle my emotions rising like a summer squall on the lake. To regain composure, I cleared my throat.

I went on after a few seconds, trying not to break down in front of my dear Jack. "Today was the auction for the rest of our belongings. As I said in my letter, we leave early in the morning."

Jack scanned the hall with one sweep of his head. Most students had already left for the weekend.

"Molly, I just want you to know I care about you." His voice broke.

Moving closer, he opened his arms. I stepped into them

as if they were a magnet drawing me. For one sweet moment, he held me. I melted in his embrace and closed my eyes for what felt like forever. If only things were different. Then, the tears began running down my cheeks. I stood there, trembling with a mountain of pent up feelings and internal sobbing. I wanted to bawl like a baby, but stopped myself with an act of sheer willpower.

"Do you want me to walk you home?" Jack asked, stepping back to look deeply into my tear-filled eyes.

Smoothing my black flannel jumper, I reached for my winter coat. How appropriate for me to be wearing black, a day for mourning. Okay, Molly, it's time to act like it was just another day at ROHS. Keep yourself together.

"Thanks, Jack. That would be sweet. Maybe you should walk me part way. Who knows what the emotional climate will be?"

"Of course. Whatever is best for you," Jack agreed.

He took my hand as we walked out of Royal Oak High School that memorable day. No need to worry about teachers reprimanding us for touching. I was no longer under their authority. Not even a little.

As we approached the block where I would go on alone, Jack stopped and turned to face me.

"Molly, you have made my senior year better than I ever imagined. Please write and let me know how you are. I promise I will write back."

He wrapped his arms around me in a gentle hug right there in front of the whole world. We stood, braced against the cold Michigan breeze, cherishing the sweetness of our first love.

"I think I'd better trudge on now, Jack," I said, pulling

slowly from his embrace. "I will write. I promise."

"I will pray for you, Molly," Jack said.

"Thanks."

I waved a last goodbye, and blew him a kiss, knowing he would watch me walk away. Now I had one more emotion to wrestle into submission. I felt such loneliness before I had even moved. My heart held so many crisscrossed feelings it was difficult to tell what hurt the most.

I dawdled on the walk home, despite the cold wind. Pulling my red hat down as close to my face as it would come, I was grateful for my snuggly wool socks and tall black boots.

I dreaded seeing our home. I didn't want to face the empty living room without my piano. I didn't want to see everything sitting in the little wooden crates. Finally reaching 606 Ninth Street, I saw the mover's truck in the driveway, partially loaded with an assortment of boxes and a few pieces of furniture.

Thankfully, Father found someone yesterday who wanted the piano, not one minute too soon. Someone in Detroit bought it for practically nothing compared to its value. At least it had a home. I was so grateful that I didn't see it roll out of sight. Thank you, Lord for sparing me.

"Hello, Molly. How did your last day go?" Father asked as I approached.

"Bittersweet," I replied. "At least I was able to tell everyone why I was about to evaporate into thin air."

Father nodded, acknowledging my words. After a solemn pause, he approached the matter at hand.

"Molly, could you please change into those work clothes your cousin Jerry gave us? He knew you could use them for the move. Would you carry the crates out so we can load them? Thanks," Father said, while continuing to arrange things. I went inside to change.

"Hi, Dear. Did you survive your last goodbyes?" Mama asked.

"I endured it," I said, shrugging. "I had a nice visit with Jack before I left. Who knows if I will ever see him again?"

"Now, now, Molly, let's keep looking up. And, who knows? Maybe there will be an even more exciting 'Jack' in Chicago," she added in a tease.

Rolling my eyes, I diverted the topic. I couldn't imagine a more exciting Jack, as Mama put it. The thought of my Jack with another girl was more than my heart could bear. I chose to distract myself with Father's request.

"Father wants me to help with loading, Mama. Where did you put the old dungarees?"

"I knew you would need something warm, and maybe even a bit ugly," she added with a chuckle. "I laid them on your bed."

"Now that's the bees' knees," I said, sarcastically.

"Now, Molly. We are all tired of this. Just go help," Mama said with a chastening tone. Lightening up, she offered a reward. "I will fix you some hot tea when you come in."

Carrying the wooden grocery crates, I soon realized how heavy they were, even packed with light items like clothing. It was a good thing I had on gloves to protect my hands, not only from the cold, but from the splinters. As I huffed in the cold, my breath exhaled wispy ice crystals into the evening air.

To be expected, supper that night was simple. Bologna sandwiches. Not exciting, but the bread was fresh. Father had several sandwiches that evening after his day of manual labor. We could eat all we wanted because the bologna wouldn't keep in the car. Not feeling particularly social, or hungry, I picked my way through part of one sandwich. The absence of routine in our now-echoing house was strange. It was no longer home.

Sleep was not easy to capture that night. I tossed, turned, twisted, and wrestled with life. We were all wide awake and dressed before the winter sun peeked out. Father's friend was there at six, ready to make his haul into Chicago and back.

"Ready to go, Molly?" Father asked, after the beds were loaded onto the truck with the last few kitchen things.

"Here, dear. Please fold and pack the sheets and blankets into the trunk of the car. We will need them handy when we get to our new place," Mama said.

Good job, Mama. It's a place, not our home. The truck had been loaded with almost everything we could take on Friday. Mama had fixed sandwiches for us to eat in the car, and more sandwiches for supper after we arrived. I wondered how many days we could live on peanut butter sandwiches. "Better than bread lines," Father would be quick to remind me.

As we pulled out of the driveway, I watched my home, the only home I had ever known, slip from view. The long drive in our rattling old Packard began. With silent tears, I settled into the backseat to sleep away as much of our nearly three-hundred-mile journey as I possibly could. The whistling wind imposed a comforting isolation from my parents. We couldn't have carried on a conversation if we had tried. However, there was nothing to say that hadn't already been said anyway. I curled up with my blanket and pillow intentionally shutting out the world. In a short while, the soothing wind-rustling sounds lulled me to sleep. I was thankful for the respite from my emotions.

"Molly, it's time for some lunch. Okay?" Mama asked, nudging me awake from the front seat.

We pulled off to the side of the road about halfway to Chicago, and ate the sandwiches Mama had prepared. She brought along a thermos of water for our drinks. I knew supper would be more of the same, but my hunger was satisfied.

Mama said we'd passed Ann Arbor and Benton Harbor already. Goodbye, Michigan. Back on the road, I watched Mama bouncing along in her seat, knitting away. Father drove, focused on the road with intensity. The scenery wasn't much to look at—winter grays, barren tree skeletons, and occasional little towns. I tried reading, but the backseat was far too bumpy for that. I had a headache anyway. Finally, I curled up on the backseat again. With the lullaby of wind resistance, I soon welcomed another retreat of sleep.

"Molly. Molly. We're home," Mama said, shaking me awake again.

I sat up. Home? What a beautiful sound. Oh, but that was not so. We were here. Not home.

"Mama, not home," I whispered. If Mama heard me, she ignored my insolence.

Father parked the car street side, and led us to the place where I would unpack my things, sleep, and eat. My parents might call it home, but it was not home. Here. In Chicago. In Lincoln Park, but as Father promised, not too far from the beach of Lake Michigan. Cold water. Windy city. Brrrrr. What did it matter if we were close to the beach? It was December.

We climbed out, stretched, and began carrying whatever we could to our third-floor apartment. We were all thankful we were not at the top of the five-story building. The truck with our furniture and boxes would arrive later, being somewhat slower than our car.

"Hank, I'm winded climbing all these stairs. I can't imagine having to carry all of our possessions up here," she added, pausing to catch her breath.

"It won't be easy, but George and I will do the heavy stuff," Father replied. He unlocked the door for us as we stood in the stuffy hallway, hands full of bedding and pillows.

"Well, it's nice and quiet here, anyway," Father said.

"And warm," I added. "Just like you said it would be." And stuffy.

Mama and I stepped inside to take our first look at where we would begin this chapter of our lives.

"Isn't this cozy?" she offered as only Mama could.

Mama was wearing her rose-colored glasses. At least the apartment was warm. Being on the third floor, the heat had risen, so our little space was toasty. I wandered back to the hallway and the two bedrooms. I could tell which room was mine right away. After my bed was in place, I would be able to take one or two steps and wham. I'd be on my bed. Cozy, Mama said. Our new place reminded me more of a vacation cabin except with indoor plumbing. I checked out our three rooms. Oh yes, and there was a teeny bathroom, half the size of ours in Royal Oak.

The living room and kitchen were together in one open room. Maybe a small table would fit between the cooking and sitting area. Probably a couple of easy chairs and our RCA Victor radio would be about the extent of living in the living room. Oh, well. I didn't usually lounge around with Mama and Father anyway. About thirty minutes later, a knock at the door signaled our belongings had arrived.

"Come in, George," Father said, ushering in the truck driver. Shortly, after showing George the small space, the men began unloading.

"Whew, this is hard work," I muttered, stomping up one flight of stairs after another to the third floor.

"I have to stop on this next landing for a few minutes and catch my breath," Mama said.

Poor Mama was not used to such exercise, even with her housework and gardening. Father either. They both looked exhausted from the whole ordeal. Within a few hours, the apartment was complete. Well, completely full. Mama and I helped carry as many crates as we could up all those flights of stairs. Unpacking boxes would wait, but George and Father set up our beds so I was grateful for that. As I prepared for bed after the very trying day, I began to sort through my rambling thoughts.

I am practical. I am a planner. Remembering Mr. Clancy's kind words, "God has a plan for you, Molly," I knew finding His will would be my quest. His promise was filled with hope. Yet I knew I was not filled with such positive inspiration. I wondered, if the whole world was upside down, how could my life ever be right side up again?

Here is my plea, Lord. Help me find your purpose for my life. I do want to find it. Whatever your will may be, please send me some hope. I don't have any of my own right now. I am watching and waiting on you, Lord.

Chapter 17—What a Holiday

Retreat! That would work. I decided that retreating would be my goal. Maybe this wasn't God's idea, but it was a way to escape my current losses. I didn't have to confront a new school for two whole weeks, so I would seek refuge in my own hidden haven. Much of my miniature world was self-created as I perched on Lilliput island. My bed.

I wrote and wrote and wrote. I had nothing but paper, a few stamps, and lots of time. I poured my heart out in letters to Jack and Winnie. I even sent one to Mr. Clancy. I maintained my sense of home through these letters.

Father had spared one luxury for us in the move, the console radio. It became my solace in the absence of music. Imagine me stuck in a world without melody and harmony except what I contrived. The radio cabinet sat in the living room, an obvious centerpiece in such a small space, a reminder of the once-looming piano in Royal Oak. But, sadly for me, not much radio programming was musical.

Nonetheless, I was grateful for the distraction. In happier times, Father, Mama, and I would listen to the radio show Chase and Sanborn. We loved to tune in their program on Sunday evenings. But not when we moved to Chicago. There was not much laughing as we each tried to find our way forward.

After the first night of camping in our walkup, as high-rise apartments were called, we gradually began to settle in. Father left early each morning, talking with business owners about work after Christmas. Mama and I had the place to clean and unpack. Since I wasn't busy with school or piano practice, I helped her set up our tiny kitchen. First, it needed a thorough cleaning.

"Here, Molly. I have the scrub brushes and vinegar water for scouring this floor."

"It is dingy-looking," I replied.

"I have just a little lemon-scented cleaner left. We can use it after we scrub off the ground-in dirt."

We brushed the grimy gray and white patterned linoleum until it had no choice but to gleam. On my hands and knees, I gave it one final wipe-down.

"I will miss that lemony cleaner, Mama. It smells so fresh, especially compared to the stinky vinegar.

"Yes, but plain vinegar and water do work, and that's what counts," Mama replied. "Vinegar only costs a few pennies."

Mama hung cute red and white checked curtains that she carried from Royal Oak for the finishing touch. Of course, the view from the windows was not much to look at—buildings and more buildings. Towers of walk-ups were all the eye could see.

The landscape of Chicago was so dissimilar from my hometown. At least, the structures around us were not run-down or dismally old. I didn't know when they had been built, but everything seemed relatively new. When winter passed, we would have to use our imaginations. Mama always grew beautiful flowers as well as vegetables galore. Next summer we wouldn't even have a porch for a flower pot.

We found a little mom-and-pop grocery store down

the street, and gathered some basics—milk, Rice Krispies, bologna, canned hash, bread, makings for soup, and such. Wisely, Father made room on the truck for several boxes of vegetables and fruit Mama had canned last summer. Having a warm meal again, no matter how simple, did my heart good.

Christmas carols played on the radio from time to time. Snow covered the ground. And, there we were, sitting in our dimly lit apartment without a tree or visible evidence of any typical Christmas traditions. We had to be creative to come up with even reminders of what we used to do. Mama gently tacked our Christmas stockings onto the windowsill in the living room—no mantel or fireplace, of course.

"Molly, help me figure out our Christmas dinner, sweetheart, will you?" she asked.

"Our stockings look sweet there, Mama. What do we have to work with for our meal?" I asked, as she finished hanging the stockings. "Can we make that delicious macaroni and cheese recipe of yours? Wasn't that Aunt Irene's original recipe? Can we get any cheese?"

"Ha-ha. You are so full of questions today. I had Father stop for some cheese, so we can make it again.

"So tasty, Mama. I remember it well."

"You're right about it being a family recipe too, originally made by your Great-Aunt Irene. Oh, and we need to cherish its creamy-cheesy goodness, especially now. Back home we paid thirty-nine cents for a pound of cheese, but here, it was forty-four cents. So, it will be a luxury."

"Well, since we're not really exchanging Christmas gifts, let's call our special meal a family present. How's that for making excuses?" I said with a laugh.

We decided on garden grown asparagus and a compote of Mama's preserved fruit. Michigan always grew the best fruits. A small baking chicken would be the treasured main dish.

"Mama, do you think you could make your world famous fudge? Do we have enough cocoa and sugar?"

"Let me check the cupboard, Molly. I did bring a small stash of staples."

I had shared the backseat with some cartons of goods Mama brought from Royal Oak.

"May I help you make it so I can learn?" I added.

"Of course, Molly. I would love to teach you."

Father knocked on the apartment door as we were setting the table that Christmas Eve. Wondering why he didn't just use his key, I opened the door with that question on my face. A wide smile spread across his face as he stood there with a scraggly little tree behind him.

"I found a Christmas tree for us," he said while dusting snow from his shoulders.

Father hadn't smiled much since we'd moved, so even this small moment of happiness was a gift. The apartment superintendent had helped Father hammer a small wooden base onto the trunk to make it stable. We sat it in the corner next to the console radio and Mama found a sheet to fluff around the platform.

"Hank, where on earth did you find this little tree on Christmas Eve?" Mama asked.

"I passed by a tree lot on the way home from my job search today. Only the saddest little trees were left, and there were only two of those," he said laughing.

"Well, we can use our imaginations, like we're doing with so many other things this year," Mama replied.

"How can we decorate it?" I asked, ignoring Mama's comment.

"We don't have much," Mama said, "but we could make some paper stars and hang them with twine or thread."

Father suggested we make some popcorn chains. We didn't have any popping corn, but Mama had some needles and thread for stringing it.

"Let's stop on our way home from church, Hank. Remember that popcorn and peanut man on the corner? He was selling popped corn for a nickel. Oh, I wonder if he will be there on Christmas Eve."

This was undoubtedly the happiest we had all been since moving to Chicago. After eating some vegetable soup, we left for the Christmas Eve service nearby. We weren't Catholic, but the grocer said St. Michael's Church was a magnificent, old historic church. He even told Mama that a sizable part of the brick structure had survived the Great Chicago Fire of 1871. The best part was we could easily walk there from our apartment building.

Even before we approached St. Michael's, we could hear the bells pealing, beckoning us to come.

"Oh, how beautiful," Mama said in awe.

Mama loved the beauty and pageantry of Christmas Eve services, regardless of where they were. My heart stirred as we walked up the steps and entered one of three impressive arched entrances. Candelabras and prayer candles flickered dancing lights onto magnificent stained-glass windows lining the sanctuary. The pipe organ's delicate flute tones permeated my senses as they drifted inside the sanctuary.

"Mama, where is the organ?" I whispered, looking all around.

Finally, after we walked far enough down the aisle, Mama pointed way up and behind us. I turned to see. The organ appeared almost in Heaven itself, sitting high above in the balcony. Its flute-like tones continued for a few minutes before the organist began playing the most familiar carol of all, "Silent Night."

We slipped into an empty row, and Mama pulled out the kneeler that was tucked below the pew. I had never been in a church like that before, but Mama knew. Her grandparents were Catholic. I sat down and closed my eyes, soaking in the beauty. Father and Mama both kneeled to pray.

A beautiful crèche sat in front of the altar, a representation of our Christian faith. As if at the second coming, trumpets heralded a new event. The priest and his attendants came down the main aisle carrying a large cross. As everyone arose from the pews, the organ played robustly, proclaiming our reason to gather together, to celebrate the birth of Jesus Christ.

Tears began to stream down my cheeks as I witnessed the pageantry and call to worship. God opened my spiritual eyes to see my self-centeredness. My heart broke. Mama put her arm around my waist, as if she had read my mind. I clung to the words from the pulpit: "The Savior—yes, the Messiah, the Lord has been born today in Bethlehem, the city of David!" The birth of Jesus had always moved me, but now, I knew all I had was brokenness.

I did not know how my life would turn out, but I knew

God spoke his love and forgiveness that evening. "I'm ready," I whispered to myself. Ready for what, I had no idea, but I promised I would give my future back to God. At the end of the service, I knew things would be different. Bring it on, Lord. Make it clear, Lord. Whatever you want for me.

Chapter 18—Christmas and Beyond

On Christmas morning, St. Michael's bells brightly proclaimed the day of celebration. I reminisced as I listened from my bed. As a little girl, I raced on tiptoes to the tree, creeping by Mama's and Father's room, in hopes of not waking them at earliest dawn. My giddiness would intensify with the discovery of each package labeled "MOLLY." This Christmas, like so many other things, would be an alteration of all previous traditions. What else would this new life impose?

Despite our attempts to lemon-fresh our place, it truly was a gloomy abode. With only a few windows and many tall buildings, the cheeriness of sunshine was limited. Oddly, I felt lost, though our intimate quarters were small. Yes, my parents were beside me, close enough to touch, but they were preoccupied. We were all trying to figure out life in this new, yet undefined dimension. I observed how we were actors again, playing out the scripts we had been handed.

On this once-glad morning, I was beckoned with a knock on my bedroom door.

"Molly, let's gather for our family celebration and breakfast," Mama called.

I struggled out of bed, with my jaw and head aching. I must have clenched my teeth all night. Golly, what a Christmas morning. When I entered the living room, Mama and Father were already seated beside our most humbly decorated tree. But it was a tree, and, it was mostly green. The three of us sat next to it with its semblance of bells, balls, and rough-cut paper chains draped on the tender branches. Sadly, we never found popcorn for a garland.

Father located some Christmas music on the old radio. What a comforting sound. I had felt some consolation and peace during the church service. For a few moments, those familiar melodies took me straight to worship. There, I was able to step outside myself and my problems to truly reflect on God's gift of Jesus.

"Here, Ruth and Molly," Father said, yanking my attention back to the moment. Reaching out his hands to mine and Mama's, he led us back to the heart of Christmas.

"Let's pray," he began.

"Father God, we want to thank you for this special time we have to consider your greatest gift of all, Jesus Christ. We are humbled by this gift you sent from Heaven. Lord, I pray you will help each of us find our way in this new place."

Deep in my heart, I knew Jesus was my only hope, but as I embraced Christmas Day, a fresh flood of reality poured over me. I could not continue to pretend it was not happening. No piano. No concert. No friends. A different high school. A big city.

"And, Lord, I pray that you will help Hank find work," Mama added. "He's a good worker, and we need your provision. We aren't asking for wealth, but for our daily bread. I also pray for Molly, as she goes to a new school, that you will bring her friends, and help her finish high school successfully. Amen."

There wasn't much to open, but we were prepared for that. I was reminded of the money Father had from my piano and winced. The move, the rent, our food–the money all had to come from somewhere. I realized we were living off the sale of my piano. I wondered how long it would last.

"Here is something important for you, Molly," Father said, handing me a small package wrapped in brown paper.

Opening it carefully, I looked with surprise at a small bundle of two-cent stamps laying in my lap. "Oh, what a perfect gift, Father," I said with genuine thanks. "Now I can mail the rest of my letters!"

Mama surprised me with a box of stationery with pretty, pink roses all around the top. She knew how important writing my friends would be, my lifeline to Royal Oak.

"Here, Ruth," Father said, handing Mama a package with dusting powder and bath salts. No wrapping paper momentarily concealed her gift, but it was apparent how grateful she was for its precious luxury.

"Oh, Hank, it smells so good. I can't wait to take a good soak with the salt. I'm still sore from all the climbing when we moved in."

Handing some envelopes to Mama and Father, I waited to see if they would be surprised with their gifts. I had made coupons for helping them around the house.

"Molly, how dear of you. It will be so nice to use your gifts of service. I can always use some help," Mama said with a generous smile.

"Hmmm … I'll save this for a time when I come home exhausted and need a little helpful chore or kind deed, Molly. Thank you," Father said.

I was relieved that we had succeeded in celebrating

Christmas in this tangible way, Hopefully, 1930 would be a better year for everyone.

"Ready for some of that service life, Molly?" Mama joked. "We need to get our breakfast together, and then on to fix a celebration dinner later. Could you beat the eggs, and just pour about a tablespoon of milk in to fluff them?"

Mama made her world-famous cinnamon muffins. Yes, they did have a touch of sweetness to them, but not as deliciously flavored with sugar as in the past. Mama placed our dishes on the small table that had once been in our garage. Of course, our nice dining room table and china cabinet didn't fit in the truck or the apartment. Father promised to try to refinish this old one, but for now it was covered with a small square of red cloth. Mama's leftover sewing scraps had come in handy once more.

After breakfast I plopped onto my bed and began writing again.

> Dear Winnie,
>
> I hope your Christmas was a good one. What was it like for you and your family? We celebrated what was "most important" last night in a beautiful, old cathedral not far from here. We were going to string popcorn for the scrawny little tree Father brought home, but—no popcorn. I cut out paper stars and hung them all around it to fill in its bald spots. Too bad I didn't have some aluminum foil to make the stars shiny. I'm learning to focus on what this holiday is really about.
>
> I'm not sure where Father found the tree, but he was pleased as punch. He managed to find us a lonely leftover on Christmas Eve. We

were all thankful. This morning we had a quiet celebration, exchanging a few presents before eating our favorite cinnamon muffins and scrambled eggs. After eating so many peanut butter and jelly sandwiches, Mama's homecooked breakfast seemed especially tasty.

Winnie, I don't have the answers to my questions, but I have talked to the Lord. Mr. Clancy said God had a plan for me. A good one, he said. Mama reminded me he was likely referring to the Scripture in Jeremiah. It tells us God wants to give us a future with hope. I am looking for his will with all my heart, Winnie. I am so hopeful I will find it.

Do you suppose God doesn't want me to play the piano after all? I can't imagine a good plan without music. Even the angels sing and play music, don't they? Do you believe God can work out this tragedy, Winnie? Oh, Winnie. I wish we could be together again, laughing and telling stories. Tell Jack hello for me. I miss seeing those sparkly, blue eyes and his big dimpled grin. Oh my. Sigh. Tears.

Love,

Molly

Before I blinked twice, the quiet days between Christmas and New Years were over. As much as I didn't want to go to school, I was dreadfully bored sitting around our apartment. I'd written Jack or Winnie almost every day, sometimes saving them to mail together. I knew my stamps would not last at such a pace. I even wrote my relatives, Aunt Lola and Grandmother and Grandfather Martin. It was snowy and bitter cold outside with no place to go and no money to spend. Father hauled out the Christmas tree. The Christmas carols stopped. It was really, in some ways, a relief. This would be a Christmas to remember, but not in the normal way.

An answer to Mama's prayers came with good news for our family. We had all counted on Father finding some temporary work. Now he would have some income from doing the books, figuring out the wreckage of a bankrupt company collapsed by debt. It wouldn't last long, but maybe other businesses going out of business would hire him. That was his hope.

For me, I would have to face the inevitable. Just as businesses wrestled with their financial failures, I would soon confront a new high school on Monday morning. I wondered what that would bring.

Chapter 19—Waller High School

Lincoln Park, Chicago

On Friday, January third, my moment of reckoning arrived. With the resolution of one walking a gangplank, I began the trek to Waller High School with Mama. No wonder Chicago has the nickname of the "Windy City." The wind howled as it plummeted between the rows of tall buildings like a wind tunnel, nearly toppling us from the sidewalk. The numbing air off icy Lake Michigan summed up my vexation. We tucked our heads down to avert the bite on our cheeks. This is only for a few months.

Classes wouldn't begin for me until Monday, which was fine. As we walked in, I felt certain that Waller had not been built anytime recently. The bricks outside appeared old, but even worse, the interior hadn't been kept up. Its decrepit structure was nothing to compare with Royal Oak's newly constructed high school. I could easily visualize the imposing entrance to ROHS—its three grand arching doors with stained glass windows as a finishing touch. Unusual for a public school, but it was considered an architectural crown jewel.

As I entered the office, I knew I was facing another revision in life. This was it. Here I come, Old Waller.

"Good morning, ma'am," the clerk said cheerily as we entered the office. A small floor heater seemed to keep the office toasty warm.

Mama spoke up. "We have just moved to Chicago, and need to enroll our daughter, Molly. She's a senior. We have her records from Royal Oak High School in Michigan," Mama explained, passing the paperwork across the counter.

I hung back, studying the bulletin board on the wall. At least it hid some of the chipped yellow paint on the faded plaster. Student clubs, sports, and after school dances were listed on a calendar for the coming semester. Apparently, they had a student orchestra because a picture was thumb tacked up there from a fall dance. The kids looked like they were enjoying themselves. Oh, Jack, if you were here, that would be loads of fun. I don't think I'll be going to any dances this spring.

"Let me get the Assistant Principal to help you with your course selection, Miss Martin. Just take a seat for a moment, please."

We looked over the course listings while we waited. I noticed they had many business training classes.

"Mama, here's the answer. If I take business classes, then maybe I can find a real job after graduation. After all, if I can't perform, what else can I do? I won't be going to a Conservatory of Music or college, so why not?"

That is, if there would be any kind of jobs after I finished school. If experienced adults couldn't get work, I knew my chances would be slim to none.

"Mama, doesn't that make sense to you too? Why would I need to take something like chemistry anyway? It is useless to me."

"But Molly dear, I always had hoped that you could go on and get some higher education," she answered softly. "Or maybe even attend a nice finishing school."

"I don't think that is relevant anymore, Mama. This is my finishing school. I just need to finish. We can't pretend we live in the world we knew even a few weeks ago."

A nice-looking young man walked in from a side office.

"Mrs. Martin and Molly, come right in. Welcome to Waller High School. I'm Mr. Robinson, principal in charge of student curriculum. I'm sure you noticed we have an old building, but we are particular about our educational standards. Because of the growth in the neighborhood since the Great War ended, we have outgrown our building. We will annex more land for construction in the future, but it won't impact what we have to offer you now," Mr. Robinson rattled on.

"I'm interested in your business courses, sir," I asserted.

I simply wanted to get this over with. Only five months to kill here and then—freedom.

"Well, let me look at your transcript here. Hmm. I see that you were not enrolled in a business curriculum at Royal Oak," he said, peering over the top of the paper at me.

"You will be underserved if you try to switch now. You have none of the business basics. What is your thinking on this?"

"I don't think my former goals will fit now. The Depression has, well, you know, Mr. Robinson. I will need a job when I graduate, if that is even possible."

"Well, it looks like your grades were mostly average. What happened here at the end?" he said, looking up curiously.

Mama chimed in before I could respond.

"Molly is very capable, Mr. Robinson, but she had

something very important to her this past year."

"And, may I ask, what that might have been?"

"I am a classical pianist, and expected to make performance my career," I replied. "I auditioned in November with the Detroit Symphony as a Young Artist."

Mr. Robinson nodded and smiled. Never asking how that turned out, he went on.

"We do have a student orchestra, Molly. They meet in the church across the street twice a week. Maybe you could help accompany them. We can check on that, now can't we?"

Imagining the music of a struggling high school orchestra, I ignored Mr. Robinson's comment like he ignored mine.

As politely as I could, I said, "Back to the business classes. May I enroll in something useful that might help me find a job? What would you suggest?"

"Well, let's see what we can do, Molly, without causing you too much grief. Remember, you missed the introductory classes."

After signing up for my final semester courses, Mama and I walked home, mostly in silence. The air was still crisp, but the wind thankfully pushed us from behind. Mama felt strongly about my education, never having encouraged me to consider marriage soon after high school. Still, her disappointment in the outlook for my future could not even begin to match my own.

After dinner, I wrote again.

Dear Jack,

I hope your holiday went well. It's hard to

think that I will be in a new high school on Monday. Well, new to me, but ugly-old. It's a large brick building that opened in nineteen hundred. I suspect there are more students here than at Royal Oak, but from what the principal said, a lot of students don't graduate. There are too many students for the building, so they're using a temporary building in the back once used for storage. I suppose I'll have to haul my coat around all day since I will have to go outside. I thought it was freezing in Michigan, but with the wind off Lake Michigan, I've already learned how brutal Chicago can be.

I enrolled mostly in business classes to finish the year—typing, shorthand (level one), and good grief, accounting, of all things. I'm drawing my sad face below for you to see. Giggle. Won't Father be amused at that. ME in accounting?! Well, I still believe the business classes are my best chance. After all, if I can't pursue my career as a musician, at least I can look for a job as a file clerk or something. Maybe I can move back to Michigan and find work next summer. That would be the best because then I can see you again. Wish you were here to enjoy the windy city of Chicago and my beautiful new high school, Jack. Jesting, of course. It won't be the same without you waiting at my locker.

Sending you hugs,

Molly

My first class on Monday was English with a Mrs. Johnson.

"Miss Martin, I'd like to introduce you to the students in English 4. Welcome."

I glanced around the room, trying to maintain a polite smile. A blur of faces stared back curiously, like gazing at a zoo animal. After class, a girl who sat across from me took time to introduce herself. I appreciated her kindness.

"Welcome, Molly. I just moved here last summer myself. Where are you from?"

"I'm from a little town outside of Detroit. Moving here was not my idea," I answered, setting the record straight right away.

"I understand," she replied. "Not mine either."

We walked together down the hall, silently at first.

Then Sarah volunteered. "I was surprised Mrs. Johnson would assign an essay on Day One after a holiday."

"At least it's only three hundred words or less," I added.

"I have no idea what I'll write about," Sarah said. "Then, to have to convince the readers why I feel so strongly will be a challenge."

"I have a feeling I will have no problem," I responded.

Sarah laughed. "I know. I'll write about why I didn't want to move to Chicago."

"Maybe I could just share my diary entries," I added, laughing with her. The very thought of showing my diary to anyone gave me shivers.

"Where do you live?" Sarah asked when we split off to find our next classes.

"Oh, we're in one of the walk-up apartment buildings about three blocks from here," I answered.

"Well, I'm not too far either. See you tomorrow. Good luck with your paper," she said.

I hurried past the abundant apartment buildings on the way home that afternoon. I imagined that the school was populated with many kids from these so-called "walk-ups." I tried to figure out how many people could fit into one building. It all seemed so foreign to me after living in the small town of Royal Oak with neighbors knowing neighbors, and abundant gardens dotting the landscape. The air was so cold my breath froze when I exhaled. Ice crystals seemed to form in my nose and mouth. Brrrrr!

I wrapped my winter coat around me as tightly as possible. As my feet pounded the brick sidewalks in their steady rhythm, my mind reverted to another time. A flood of memories washed over me. Music was still alive in me. I began humming the parts I had played with such devotion only weeks ago. As clearly as if it were yesterday, Rachmaninoff's brilliant theme spilled its passion like a balm for my troubled spirit. I had tried to smother it in the past two weeks, unsuccessfully.

My heart beat faster as I recalled the most beautiful experience ever in my short lifetime. As I climbed the stairs to our apartment, I felt a rush of gratitude. I would forever be grateful for my one opportunity to play Rachmaninoff with the symphony.

Lord, is it selfish to ask if I can play again?

I pulled out the door key string buried under my coat, sweater, and blouse. We couldn't leave our place open like we did back home, so I had to unlock to get in.

"Click. Click. Mama? I'm back."

"Oh, good, Molly. Do you have homework to do tonight, or did they start you off easy?"

"I have to memorize the keyboard, Mama," I said

laughing. "Not the piano keyboard, of course. I've already got that, right? I need to learn the placement of the letters on the typewriter. I also have to start learning the shorthand symbols."

"Well, that will be easy-peasy for you, I would say," she joked.

"Oh, I forgot to mention that I also have an essay to write for English. Can you believe it?"

"Well, change clothes and relax. If you want to turn on the radio, you can. I'm about to fix us some beef for supper." Then, she added, "Chipped beef over toast?" Mama asked with her inimitable grin.

"Yes, Mama," I groaned. "Not a favorite, but I will say you make it as tasty as anyone could."

I took one step into my room's four walls, and plopped on the bed. I'd never wanted a twin bed, but it was too bad I didn't own one now. I had to laugh at myself. That's what I get for being an only child. The luxury of a double bed, and a room of my own. Lucky kid? Well, I don't think I'd go that far, but at least I did still have a sense of humor.

Day ONE of the rest of my school days was behind me. I met one nice girl, and Rachmaninoff ran through my head like a haunting melody. How could such magnificent beauty simultaneously cause so much torment?

What would day two look like? I decided to make a countdown chart until I finished my "finishing school," as I teased with Mama. I needed to finish, and then see what God has in store. Maybe I could go back and work in Royal Oak. Maybe I would even marry handsome Jack, after all. Who knew the answer? Only God.

Chapter 20—The Birth of a Plan

What now? Mrs. Johnson doesn't even know me, yet she stopped me after class. I did my homework. I haven't been at Waller long enough to have any grades—good, bad, or otherwise.

"Molly, may I have a word?"

I turned, likely wearing a giant question mark on my face. I couldn't imagine what she wanted. Did Mr. Hill write? Mind your beeswax, Professor Bunsen Burner. This is my new beginning.

"I read your essay last night." Mrs. Johnson paused as if she wasn't sure what to say. "You have quite a story, Molly."

Whew. I melted with relief to discover I wasn't in trouble. I didn't know how to respond to her. I just stood there, feeling embarrassed for the attention.

"Could you stop by after school today?" she said.

Oh, goodness. All day, I wondered what Mrs. Johnson wanted with me. I had to try to attend to my classes in the meantime. In shorthand class, I learned a few more symbols. It was actually interesting, sort of like using a private code. It reminded me of the secret symbols Winnie and I made up years ago, so we could pass notes in privacy. That memory made me laugh inside. Oh, Winnie, I wish you were here now.

The students in my business classes were friendly enough to say hello, but nobody had really talked to me, except

Sarah in English. She was in the orchestra, so maybe if I did decide to accompany, I would see her more. But, the thoughts of a beginning student orchestra didn't motivate me. I think I might be a musical snob. Quite probably true.

My inner thoughts were abruptly interrupted when I heard my name.

"Molly? Could you please explain the difference between basic terms 'accounts receivable' and 'accounts payable'?"

After clearing my throat, I managed to respond. It was awkward being the center of attention as the new student. What if you messed up and that's what everyone remembered about you?

"I believe accounts payable refers to something a business owes, like a debt. And, then accounts receivable would be the money collected for its services."

"Correct. Can you apply this knowledge to businesses today, rightly reeling from the Crash?" Mr. Schecter asked.

"I think so. My father often talks about it. He says businesses have too many accounts payable. Since their customers don't have any money, they aren't able to collect on the services they've provided," I answered quietly.

"Very good. Simple and clearly stated," he responded smiling. "Tell your father he's done a good job of explaining the facts."

"So, as I understand it," I said with added confidence, "this means businesses don't have any assets to offset their debts."

I was reasonably satisfied with my answer, not because I had studied so hard, but because Father was an accountant. He had used all these terms when talking about the businesses failing.

"You have accurately described the plight of businesses lacking financial flow, Molly. Thank you for studying," Mr. Schecter replied.

Flashing back to Mr. Hill, I smiled, remembering how he never thanked students for anything. What a mean old egg he was.

In my effort to acquire some practical skills, the business courses were certainly on the mark. In typing class, we learned how to properly set up a business letter and were tested on remembering the location of the keys on the typewriter g, j, i, s, and l. Thrilling. I tried to visualize myself as a receptionist in an office. That was hardly the excitement of being seated at a grand piano in a concert hall. But this was real life, and I was trying to make peace with it.

At last, the bell rang. I hurried back up to the fourth floor. I could not begin to imagine what Mrs. Johnson would say. As I entered the classroom, slightly out of breath, Mrs. Johnson stood up from her desk and smiled warmly. I was thankful for her kind expression.

"Molly, thanks for coming back this afternoon when I know you're anxious to get home. From your essay, it sounds like you've been through a tumult of emotions over the past few months. Before I say anything else, congratulations on your acceptance as a Young Artist Performer. What an honor. Remind me again, Molly. When is the concert?"

"January 25, ma'am."

"So, you have a little more than two weeks left?"

"Yes, ma'am, but I'm not able to perform. In fact, we still need to let the symphony know because everything happened so fast. I kept hoping and praying something would work out. You see, I don't have a piano anymore." I paused. "I also don't have transportation back to Detroit."

"I may be able to help with one part of this, Molly. The church across the street has a room where our students attend orchestra. What if I could arrange for you to practice there?"

"Gee, really? That would be wonderful," I said. Were my ears tricking me? A piano?

"Do you want to go over now to see if we can schedule a practice time?" she asked.

"Sure," I answered without hesitation. I didn't think Mama would worry. It was still daylight. We walked over to the Presbyterian Church, and Mrs. Johnson led into the office.

"Is Pastor Thomas available?" she asked. "I'd like to introduce him to one of our new students. Molly recently transferred from a small community outside of Detroit."

"Of course. Let me see if he's available," she said.

We waited while the secretary located the pastor. Within a few minutes, a bespectacled man with a congenial face appeared.

"Well, Mrs. Johnson. How nice to see you again. Is everything running smoothly with the orchestra schedule?"

"Yes, Pastor, everything is fine. We're so grateful the orchestra can use your space. As you know, Waller is overflowing."

Reaching for my hand, Mrs. Johnson announced, "Pastor Thomas, I'm here today for another matter. I'd like to introduce Molly Martin, a new senior with us."

"Welcome to the city of Chicago," he said with gusto.

"Molly's family just moved here from Royal Oak over Christmas," Mrs. Johnson added.

"Pleased to meet you, Molly." Pastor Thomas extended his hand to shake mine.

"Thank you, Pastor. Chicago is quite different from my small hometown, but I'm trying to learn its ways."

Honestly, that was not true, but it sounded positive. I didn't want to offend him since he seemed so warm and welcoming.

Mrs. Johnson continued.

"I recently learned Molly is a gifted pianist. She earned the privilege of playing a Rachmaninoff Concerto with the Detroit Symphony—the Young Artist audition winner for 1929."

"Congratulations on your hard work and success," Pastor Thomas replied.

"Well, here is the big picture, Pastor," Mrs. Johnson added. "The concert is scheduled for later this month, but Molly's family had to move here because of her father's job loss."

"I'm sorry," he answered. "Will you still be able to perform?"

"No," I responded. "I don't even have a piano now."

Pastor Thomas appeared moved by that news. He looked down as if deliberating his next words.

"It sounds like you have been through a lot recently. I know that must be difficult. So many of our families are experiencing hard times."

"When I heard of Molly's predicament, I thought of you and your generosity toward our students. I wonder if it would be possible for Molly to practice on the church piano for the next couple of weeks? You don't have to answer today."

"I can answer now," the pastor said. "We would be delighted to have Molly use the piano. Come, and I'll show you what we have. It's not a stage grand, of course."

We walked back to a room where there was an old upright piano, a Baldwin Acrosonic. I ran my fingers up and down, and played a few chords. The keys flew beneath my strong hands. Though the feather light touch compared to the grand's weighted keys was not the best, I didn't care. IT WAS A PIANO. I was beaming inside and out. A piano!

"I know it's a bit out of tune," said Pastor Thomas, "but it does have strings. All the keys still play."

"Oh, please don't apologize. My teacher, Mr. Clancy in Royal Oak, taught me that the Russian composer, Stravinsky, loved Baldwin pianos. I studied Stravinsky's 'Russian Dance' with Mr. Clancy last year. Oh, do excuse me. I'm babbling now. I'm so grateful for this opportunity. Thank you, thank you, thank you," I said, hardly stopping for breath.

"What should I tell the secretary about your schedule?" he asked.

"Oh, I will be here every day after school," I answered. "I just need to tell my parents this wonderful news. I'm sure they will support me."

As we said our polite goodbyes, I wanted to jump up and down with joy. At least my heart was leaping, even while my feet remained firmly planted. All the way home, my spirits soared. Was I really going to play again? Could I possibly, somehow, get back to Detroit to perform with the symphony?

Climbing up the three flights of stairs two steps at a time, I entered the apartment breathless. I couldn't wait to share my news. I believed this was God working things out.

"Mama," I called, not seeing her as I walked in. "I have exciting news!"

"Oh, my," she said, coming from her bedroom. "Thank goodness, you're home. I was beginning to worry because it's later than usual."

"Mama, you will never fancy what happened. All day, I wondered what Mrs. Johnson wanted to tell me. I couldn't even imagine this outcome," I blurted out.

"Who is Mrs. Johnson?" she asked.

"My English teacher who assigned the essay. I couldn't figure out why she asked me to come in after school. After all, I handed in my paper on time."

Every sentence rose in volume as I spoke. Finally, I blurted out at the top of my voice, "I can practice the piano again!"

"Slow down, Molly. What are you talking about?" Mama asked.

"There's a piano in a church across the street from school, and my English teacher took me over to see the pastor, and he said I could practice after school, so maybe I can still play with the symphony on January 25, and aren't you excited for me?" I exclaimed in a nonstop stream.

Mama stared in amazement.

"Why, yes. We should thank the Lord for answering your prayers," she said.

"I know he has, Mama. I know he has. Mr. Clancy and

you both said God had a good plan for me. Isn't this perfect? I know it will work even though the piano is an out-of-tune Acrosonic with baby-light keys. May I tell them tomorrow that I can stay after school?"

"We'll talk to Father tonight. We have to figure out how to get you back to Detroit if you're able to practice again."

"I know this will work, Mama," I said. "I just know this is how God is working things out."

"Transportation costs money, you know," Mama cautioned.

That brought me back to the moment, but I remained optimistic. After all, how could that stop me now that the Lord had opened this door?

At dinner, Mama and I shared the unexpected opportunity with Father. He seemed blindsided to learn I might be able to perform.

Father's face was soft and kind as he soaked in the news. There was a long silence while he contemplated the larger question of transportation.

"This is incredible news. We will have to see where this may lead."

He was smiling though. A very good sign, I was sure.

If we drove to the concert in the car, Father would have to miss work, and that would make it even more expensive. After dinner, Father went to his bedroom while Mama and I began washing the dishes. Returning with something in his hands, Father carefully opened a white envelope. My eyes opened wide.

"Molly, I set aside a few dollars from the piano sale. We'll keep this separate from our other funds to cover your travel expenses," Father said.

"Thank you, Father!" I said. I wiped my hands quickly, and threw my arms around him.

"Now I will have to research the best way to get you to Detroit and the cost," Father said.

I had never really trusted my earthly Father would get me back to Detroit. But, lo and behold, my Heavenly Father was tearing down the obstacles, one by one. I was certain of that.

After the dishes were done, I went to my room to "tell" Winnie about this development. Paper and pen. Envelope and stamp. It was the only way we could keep our friendship intact.

> Dear Winnie,
>
> You'll never guess what happened today. I have a piano to practice on and a train ticket may be in my future for the January concert! I don't know the outcome yet, but I believe God is working. Please pray with me that I will get back for the concert. Will I? Won't I? I don't know, but I continue to pray.
>
> Miss you so much, dear friend. Friends forever and ever.
>
> Love,
>
> Molly

Chapter 21—Preparations

I was desperate to see Mrs. Johnson Friday morning. Rushing through the halls so I wouldn't be late, I burst into her room like a Kansas twister. She was writing on the chalkboard, but looked up, happy to see me.

"Mrs. Johnson, please forgive me for interrupting your work. I will take only a moment."

"Good morning to you. What's on your mind?" she said.

"I have good news. My parents agreed for me to practice after school, and they have even set aside the money so I can go to Detroit for the concert. Isn't this marvelous? I didn't even know my father had any money."

"Oh, Molly, that is absolutely wonderful. I will set it up today so you can start Monday."

She had the most genuine smile on her face. I went into the hallway to wait for the bell to ring. I felt the urge to tell someone my news. But I didn't know many anyones. At last, I saw Sarah coming. She would understand. Of course, she would.

"Hi, Sarah. I have some good news."

"That's nice to hear, Molly, and I love to see your happy smile today."

"Let's get seated, boys and girls. It's time to begin," Mrs. Johnson announced, drawing us inside.

While Mrs. Johnson took attendance, I passed Sarah a note. She quickly scrawled something, and handed it back: "Meet me at locker 277 on the second floor after school, if you can."

I nodded in assent, and turned to respond as Mrs. Johnson called my name for the roll.

"Miss Martin?"

"Present," I answered promptly.

It seemed so long since my afternoon meetings at the lockers back home. Oh, Winnie and Jack, I know you will be so happy for me. Letters are so slow, and you cannot see and hear reactions. Good news is meant to be shared. Remembering when I bared my soul on my darkest days, I knew sad things must be shared too.

When the last bell of the day rang, I was so ready to spill my news. I thought I would explode with the excitement building inside of me.

"Hi, Sarah! Thanks for waiting for me. I hurried as fast as I could. I know it's Friday and we're both ready to beat it out of here."

"Tell me your news, Molly. You look happier than I've seen you since we met the first day."

"Sarah, did I ever explain why we moved here?"

"Not really. I figured it had to do with the Depression since so many people are struggling," Sarah answered.

"My father lost his job. I know you play in the orchestra, so maybe you will understand how I feel about music."

"Ha, ha," Sarah began laughing. "That's a funny combination of ideas. What does music have to do with your father's job?"

"Gee, Sarah, there is so much to tell you. In short, music was the center of my life. I auditioned to play a piano concerto with the Detroit Symphony at the end of January. Yet, I am here. Even worse, they had to sell my beloved piano."

"Oh, golly. I had no idea you were so talented. How are you managing without going completely blooey? That's just horrible. For crying out loud, how are you handling school at all?" Sarah exclaimed.

Sarah's short blonde hair framed her lightly freckled face. The more excited she became, the more animated her expressions were.

"I've had my down times, for sure. Here's the bee's knees though," I said, laughing at the humor as I said it. "Mrs. Johnson has gotten permission for me to practice at the church. And, even better, my parents are helping me get back to Detroit for the concert which is January 25! I can't believe how this is coming together when I had completely given up hope."

"How exciting, Molly. That is the 'cat's whiskers,'" Sarah added with a tease. "Would it be all right if I come over to listen?" she asked.

Sarah reminded me of the "five-foot-two-eyes-of-blue" kind of girl. The kind I always wanted to be, not the skinny, tall bean I was.

"Of course, Sarah." I answered. "Give me a few days to practice. It's been weeks since I've even touched the keys. Okay?"

"Just let me know when you're ready. I volunteer to be your practice audience. I really can't even imagine listening to a live piano concerto," Sarah said.

On the way home, I sang, and prayed, and felt so joyful. I didn't even have words to put it all together.

"Mama? I'm home. I have even more good news."

"It's so good to have you home for the weekend with a smile on your face again. What good news did you bring today?"

"I spoke with Mrs. Johnson, and she is setting it up for me to practice starting Monday. I can hardly wait to have piano keys under these fingers again."

Mama smiled and nodded. I believed she understood my heart.

"And, Mama, I simply had to tell someone today. A person with a body and face—besides you and Father, of course." I laughed as Mama did.

"I wanted to tell someone who is here. Someone who would care. I thought I would explode with such good news bottled up all day. And, you know what? God gave me that very person."

"Who did you tell, Molly?"

"Remember the girl who took the time to introduce herself to me? Her name is Sarah. She's in English with me, but she also plays in the orchestra. I thought maybe, just maybe, she might care about music enough to understand."

"And did she?" Mama inquired.

"Yes, she did. She even asked how I could stand to attend school with everything going on. Even better than that, she asked if she could listen to me some afternoon."

I could feel my smile transform my face, and it felt so amazing to be happy again.

On Saturday, we checked the train schedules from

Chicago to Royal Oak. Father thought trains would be safer than buses. I didn't care. I only wanted to get there. The trip details materialized. Mama and I could ride the elevated train to Union Station, so Father wouldn't miss any work that Friday afternoon. The 'L,' as it was called, had many routes in and around Chicago that ran all day and night.

Mama made a long-distance phone call to Winnie's parents. It had to be quick because the cost was prohibitive. Every minute, it was compounded, making each additional minute more expensive than the one before.

"Hello, Maggie," Mama began. "It's so good to hear your voice again. We have some good news, and a big favor to ask."

I could tell Mama didn't encourage more conversation than necessary, but I knew Winnie's mom would understand.

Winnie's parents were gracious, offering for me to stay with them. Even if they were unable to drive me to Detroit on Saturday, they promised to take me to the interurban streetcar in Royal Oak. The same one Mama and I had ridden.

On one hand, I was hopeful and excited. On the other hand, I was a teeny bit anxious. How would everything turn out? It seemed that God was breaking down the most impossible barriers. Was my dream still feasible? I knew God could make it happen.

On Sunday, my parents and I visited a different church. Coincidentally, the pastor's sermon was the apropos topic of spiritual peace—how to acquire it, how to keep it. He caught my attention because I certainly had trouble living in peace. I couldn't seem to hang on to peace. It kept slipping away at every possible new situation. I crawled out of my personal tunnel of thoughts just in time to hear the message.

"In John 14:27," he boomed, "God speaks to us about giving us His peace, even in troubled times."

What a contradiction. How could I have peace in trouble?

"Peace I leave with you, my peace I give unto you: not as the world giveth, give I unto you," the pastor read from his hefty pulpit Bible. "Let not your heart be troubled, neither let it be afraid."

Okay, so I wasn't afraid, I argued. After all, I now had a piano to play. We even had a way for my transportation. I had a place to stay. I decided, then and there, to grab hold of God's peace and remain positive. God was working out his will for me.

Sunday afternoon, I pulled out my favorite Parker pen and began sharing with Jack again.

> Dear Jack,
>
> I am so excited! A teacher at my new school learned about my situation through a welcome-back-to-school-essay. You know, one of those assignments where they tell you to write about your deepest-held convictions. Only this time, I unloaded. I really wrote a Tell All paper. Mama would say I was wearing my heart on my sleeve (or on my English paper). In this case, at least I got a grade out of it. Laughing here. I had nothing to lose so I wrote everything that had happened since Father lost his job. Well, maybe not everything. That might be overwhelmingly embarrassing.

Within a couple of days, that nice teacher had a piano lined up. She arranged for me to practice after school at a nearby church. Isn't that tremendous? I had been feeling so cut off. Helpless to make anything happen. Even though I knew you and others cared, I didn't see any solutions. Now I can practice again, and believe it or not, Father is helping me pay for a train ticket. Such an irony. He had to sell my piano, yet the old family piano is now funding my transportation to Detroit. God does work in mysterious ways, as the old hymn goes.

I will arrive on Friday afternoon, January 24, on the Grand Trunk Western rail line. I'm supposed to rehearse with the symphony Friday evening, so I won't be able to see you then. The concert is a matinee at 1:30, Saturday. It would be so nifty if you could come. If not, maybe I can see you on Saturday evening or Sunday before I return home. I'm staying with Winnie. You can call me there. Her number is "583J."

With love,

Molly

PS Write back as soon as you can."

As I prepared for sleep, I prayed.

Lord God, it seems you are working things out for my good, and I thank you. I truly do want to trust you with my dreams. What will the future hold, Lord? Only you know. I wait to see how you will work. Amen.

Chapter 22—A Collision with Reality

January 24! It arrived right on time. I had practiced hard for two weeks, rehearsing daily. Mr. Clancy's rigorous training had provided a strong musical foundation from which I could rebound. Mama came over to the church every afternoon to walk me home in winter's twilight. Even Father was patient about supper being late most days. For me, life couldn't have turned a more hope-filled corner, and I was grateful.

I was as ready to perform as possible in this new rendition of my life. Mama trimmed my hair bob the best she could using her sewing scissors. My favorite red crepe "silhouette style" dress was packed, along with red heels and my only pair of silk stockings. I would have to be careful not to catch a run or snag or I'd be bare-legged on stage. The dress had a circular skirt, with just a touch of swing at the hemline. Thankfully, some shirring and tucks on the bodice were a nice distraction from my narrow shape.

All three of us seemed to feel the excitement of this grand event. Thursday night at dinner, Father started telling us about Union Station where he'd purchased my tickets.

"I can't wait until you see Chicago's train depot," Father said. "The lobby is called the Great Hall. Extraordinary. I bought your round-trip ticket so I guess everything is all set. You and Mama will have to be on time for your departure at ten."

"Don't worry about that part," I said, giggling. "I've

packed and will be ready to leave first thing in the morning," I said.

I looked forward to seeing the station for myself, riding the train alone, and all the rest to follow. Sleep did not come easy that night. The only thing that could make my dream more complete would be to have Mama, Jack, Winnie, and Mr. Clancy at the concert. And, Father too. I had to admit he was trying to be a good stepfather. I knew in my head the Depression was the reason he lost his job which caused everything else. But, separating Father from my own losses was not easy. I had forgiven him for selling my piano and making us move. But, maybe, deep inside, that forgiveness was a work in progress.

As I lay there tossing and turning, the concerto spun around in my mind, just like it did when I auditioned. I never minded reliving its enthralling melody, except ... well, maybe it was not as welcome when I needed to fall asleep.

"Thank you, Lord," I whispered, as I eventually relaxed. My mind slowly shut down.

I woke up early to see enormous fat snowflakes wafting to the ground. With hopes of the fulfillment of a dream—my dream—no snow could stifle my joy. Open the skies and unload the heavens. A snowy blanket across Chicago and all of Michigan would not chill my mood. Father delivered us to Union Station with time to spare. He dropped us off at the curb, and left us with smiles and good wishes.

"I know you will do your best," Father said, waving us off. "Ruth, call me after Molly gets on the train, and I'll come back for you."

Mama and I brushed the snowflakes off our coats and

boots as we approached the entrance to Union Station. We were about an hour early, so we would have time to explore the Great Hall Father had described. I spun around on the gleaming marble floors and gazed up to the spacious five-story, vaulted ceiling.

Oh, goodness gracious. This ornate structure was a sensory experience, not a train station. It was truly glorious.

Huge American flags hung majestically from the balconies. The structure flaunted soaring Corinthian columns stretching toward skylights. Such luxury seemed to mock those of us who were scraping up our pennies to buy a single train ticket. In 1925, no one in America could have imagined the kind of poverty we were experiencing now.

We walked over to the schedule boards to find where I needed to be. Scanning the many listings, I didn't see my train route posted.

"Mama, do you see my train schedule?" I asked.

"No, Molly, I'm looking for it too. In fact, I wonder. Oh, no. Look over there. Do you see the list?"

Posted by cities and times we saw cancellation after cancellation. I picked up my satchel and walked to the desk to speak with a ticket agent.

"Sir, I have a round trip ticket to Detroit, which was supposed to leave at 10. I see that it has been cancelled. I must, and I mean must, be in Detroit by tonight."

"I'm sorry, Miss, but a lot of routes have been cancelled today. Between the heavy snow and the shortage of passengers, things have about come to a stop."

"I have to be there this evening for a rehearsal," I said with a bite in my voice.

"See all these other people? I can't help you, Miss. Next in line …"

"Wait a minute," I said more insistently. "I have a round trip ticket right here. Aren't you going to at least refund my money?"

"Well, if money weren't the problem right now, we'd have the trains all running, Miss. Try another day. Maybe the Grand Trunk Western will be running their normal schedule," he answered hastily. "Your ticket will still be good."

I turned to where Mama was standing, feeling as if I had just been slapped in the face.

"How can this be?" I asked. Quickly, I started thinking of alternatives. There had to be another way to get there.

"What about a bus, Mama? Can't we buy a bus ticket? I will ride the bus, even if there are more transfers, and it takes longer."

"I don't have any money, Molly. Father used over twenty dollars of savings to buy your round-trip ticket."

"Call Father. Surely, he can work this out," I insisted.

"Let's call Winifred's mother first and let her know you aren't arriving on time," she said.

We walked to a pay phone on the other side of the Great Hall. Mama fished in her purse to realize she didn't have enough change for a long-distance call. I sat down on one of the oversized benches. That even made me feel even more insignificant—small as a ladybug in a snowstorm. I couldn't grasp what just happened.

What are You doing, Lord? I thought you were working things out. My dream should not end like this. This could not be all to the story.

Tears welled up and slowly trickled down my cheeks. I felt I was suffocating. Please God. Please God. Please God. I begged with every fiber of my being, though panic shackled me.

Chapter 23—My Blizzard

With every step out of the station, I agonized. Each footstep plunged heavily into the deepening snow. Still in denial, I refused to accept the destiny I beheld.

"Mama, I can't leave this alone. I've come too far, and there must be another way to get me to Detroit."

"Now, Molly, I've explained we don't have time, or money, for alternatives."

Stomping along like an insolent two-year-old, I let Mama have it.

"Mama, you've simply resigned yourself. Just like that," I said, trying to snap my fingers in my bulky gloves. "You're not even trying to creatively solve this problem."

"No, Molly, you're wrong. There are times when we have to face reality," Mama said with a firmness uncommonly heard from her lips.

"I will not give up. I am playing with the symphony tomorrow even if I have to walk there."

My frustration boiled so thick that even the frigid air could not quench the raging fire within. I spun around to face Mama.

"Mama, just take the 'L' by yourself. I'm going to walk to the apartment."

"Molly, that is silly. Walking in a blizzard will not get you one inch closer to Detroit."

"I don't care. This whole thing is nuts," I said, crossing to the opposite side of the street.

Mama stood watching, but I quickly disappeared around the corner. I believed I could get home on foot. It was surely not that many blocks. Anyway, I had a lot to sort out, and Mama wasn't helping a bit.

I walked for a few blocks, past stores and buildings which were rapidly cloaked in purest white. Chicago seemed more hospitable covered in its new frosty blanket. I remained confident of my internal compass, but quickly, the blocks grew indistinguishable. I shoved my hands deeper into my pockets, and trudged onward fearlessly. Head down to protect my face, I wrangled with Omnipotent God and my own disillusionment. Where was my breakthrough? Where was his all-powerful self now?

"So, Lord, could you please explain how this good plan of yours works?"

Looking upward into the plume of white on white, I vented aloud. A few people turned their heads to see who was yelling, but I didn't care. Thankfully, people were hurrying to get out of the weather. No one bothered me.

"God, don't you hear my prayers? How can I walk according to your purposes with all these obstacles?"

I hollered up into the snowy sky while kicking at the growing accumulation on the sidewalk. I passed a corner newsstand and the Detroit Free Press jumped out at me. It was stacked alongside the Chicago Tribune, and the New York Daily among other city newspapers. I went back for a second look. I quickly scanned one of the Chicago headlines: "Mob Feuds Continue Despite Capone's Stay in Miami." I glanced around looking out for a mobster-type that might be lurking nearby. Even in my anger, I had to laugh at my reaction. A mob shootout would be a perfect topping for my day.

I touched the corner of the Detroit paper with my nearly frozen fingers and read: "City Struggles with Huge Job Losses." In smaller bold-faced print: "Detroit Symphony Makes Brutal Cuts." Fine. Now even the symphony is being destroyed. Just like Father predicted.

Walking away from the newspapers, I hurried to the next street light and took a left. Looking up and down the busy intersection, I wondered if maybe I should go back and turn right. Everything looked the same now—white. In my tantrum, I hadn't paid close enough attention to where I was going. Of course, the wind was now creating drifts along the streets and store fronts.

By now my fingers were numb and I couldn't feel my toes at all. Was Mama home by now? Maybe I should call Father. Who to call—who to call? I would be in trouble with both parents by now. Stubborn enough to prove I could find my way home, I decided not to call Father. He'd just be angry. Or even Mama. What could she do anyway?

I had some loose change in my purse. Maybe I had enough for a local call. I entered a drugstore to inquire about a pay phone. The warmth was a comfort to my freezing limbs. I took my hat and gloves off, and blew on my fingers to revive them.

"Mister, could you tell me if I'm anywhere close to Lincoln Park?" I asked.

"Well, Lincoln Park is still quite a hike from here, Miss," he said. "You can count the new streetlights to help. They were just installed this past year," he said boasting proudly as if he had made the decision himself. "They have sure helped with all the autos on the roads these days."

The clerk told me I had about eight or more cold and snowy blocks yet to go. Turn this way, and then that way, then down two lights, and on and on he went.

After all of that, I went over to the soda fountain to sit for a minute.

"May I help you?" the waitress asked.

I was tempted to order a hot drink. Yet caution prevailed. I knew I might need that little bit of money. Maybe when Father heard, maybe he did have enough money to get a round trip bus ticket. Even if I missed the rehearsal tonight, I could still get there by tomorrow afternoon. We could call the symphony director and explain everything.

"No, thank you," I said. "I just need to warm up for a minute and then hurry home."

"Yes, you should get out of this weather, young lady. You know, the Farmer's Almanac says we're in for a hard winter, and this looks like a good taste."

The waitress chattered on as if that was the most important news of the day. I bundled up again to begin my final trek home. At least I had directions now. I felt some stinging on my cheeks, realizing I would certainly be wind burned. Hopefully, my fingers wouldn't get frostbite. I snuggled them into a fist in my pockets and continued face down. The snow pelted against me like icy darts.

Would Mama possibly understand why I was so angry, even if this wasn't her fault? Probably not. Nobody would. Maybe not even God.

As I rounded the last corner and saw our building in the distance, I was thrilled to know I'd made it. Yet, I dreaded what was next.

Chapter 24—The Death of a Dream

Mama's red swollen eyes and Father's angry glare met me as I stepped through the door. With fingers tightly entwined, they sat at ramrod attention. Father's countenance was unbearable. Mama's sadness permeated the room.

Father stood, raising his voice to such volume I could only hope the neighbors didn't hear. "Young lady, do you have even a tiny notion of the fear you stirred up in your mother? Such irresponsibility! Do you realize we called the police to report you missing?"

Mama started blubber-talking with words wrapped in tears, all spilling over at once.

"Molly, I was desperate. There you were, out in a blizzard, walking around a dangerous city you don't know, angry at the world," she began. "Why did you do this? Did the symphony concert become more feasible as you wandered around Chicago?"

"I needed time to think, Mama. I didn't intend to hurt you," I said quietly. "You didn't seem to understand, and I had a lot of figuring out to do. I am nearly an adult, you know. In another few months, I'll be out of high school. I didn't think walking home would be such a big problem."

"Young LADY!" Father said, raising his voice another octave, and glaring in my direction.

They did not like my defense, so I walked to my place of solace, defeated, and quivering from the cold. With winter's grip still clutching me, I curled up in the fetal position with covers piled over my head. How fitting. I couldn't have felt more miserable if Father had physically beaten me. As I lay there, my anger transitioned to tears. The floodgates opened.

I give up. On everything. Myself, my dreams, my parents. Maybe even God Himself.

At last, I could not cry one more tear, and eventually drifted off to sleep. About three o'clock, the shrill ring of our telephone woke me. We didn't receive many calls, so I tiptoed to my door and listened.

"Yes, Maggie, this is Ruth. Thank you for calling back. We can't get Molly to Detroit as we'd hoped. Between the trains having trouble filling their cars with paying fares and our blizzard conditions …"

There was a long silence.

"Is that right?" Mama added. "No, we didn't receive a letter or a phone call. How strange that Molly wouldn't have been notified. That seems irresponsible."

After Mama hung up, she tapped on my door.

"Molly, would you please come out? We need to talk."

I grabbed my robe and went out to see what was going on.

"The concert tomorrow has been cancelled," Mama said.

"What? How could that be?" I countered.

"Why no one had the courtesy to let you know is beyond me. Winnie's parents saw a writeup in the Detroit Free Press only this morning."

"I saw a newspaper headline saying the symphony is

having financial problems. Just like Father said it would."

"They had to scale back their schedule because not enough patrons have purchased tickets. But why didn't they notify you? It seems so inconsiderate to treat a young musician like that," Mama went on, almost talking to herself about the matter.

After a somber pause, a possible explanation came to mind. "Mama, I don't think I ever told the symphony we were moving. It all happened so fast. Did you?"

"No. We had too many things to do before the move." A shocked expression crossed Mama's face.

"Then, if they sent a letter, it is probably in the lost mail or sitting in our old mailbox," I said. "Even if they called, our phone was disconnected."

What a melodrama. I knew which mask I would wear if I were acting. To add to my grief, the miscommunication was my fault. How would they know we had moved? I walked back to my cozy hideaway. My dream was finished. That's all there was to it. Over. Done. I could not have written a more sorrowful plot in a novel.

My faith was shattered. My body was spent from all my emotional spewing. This whole journey had been nothing but a series of mountaintops and valleys. In despair, I turned to the Lord, the only one who could take away my pain.

God, I know you are the creator of all things. I know you can turn situations around and use them for our good. But I see nothing good coming from any of this.

As I wallowed in my hopelessness, I remembered learning the twenty-third Psalm as a child. Mama and I practiced it line by line, night after night.

"Yea, though I walk through the valley of the shadow of

death …" Yes, that's what this feels like, Lord. The valley of dead dreams.

"Thou art with me …"

God, are you still with me?

Okay. I'm going to make a choice. With an act of my will, I choose to believe you are still with me though I don't see you.

I fought back more tears.

Chapter 25—It's Not for You or Me

Tension. Raw suffocating tension. The next morning, at best, we were awkwardly civil with our words. I felt sure that anger commingled with a dab of empathy in each of us. In Royal Oak, I fled the house because of our move to Chicago. In Chicago, I would have welcomed an escape after my direct defiance.

I had never been what some would call a rebellious child. I was nearly eighteen, yet still a dependent, which certainly established the framework for our relationships. I had to obey as long as I lived there. I could hear Father saying, "As long as you eat my food, and put your feet under my table, you will obey our rules."

I needed a to figure out how to navigate in these rough waters. Okay then, for the short term, my attention would be to simply finish school. In May, I could graduate. February, March, April, and May. That's all I had left. I could do this.

Surprised by my own change of heart, I truly couldn't wait to get back to classes on Monday. Mrs. Johnson was waiting for a word of presumed excitement as I walked in that day.

"No. You don't say, Molly," she remarked in disbelief. "I knew you were taking the train, so I assumed you had made it, despite the snowstorm."

She was even more stunned when I explained that the

concert had been cancelled.

"Molly, you can still practice at the church any time while you are enrolled here," she said. "Piano can still be a part of your life whenever you want it."

When I saw Sarah in English, I didn't feel like going through the whole drama again.

"Was your trip amazing?" she asked, almost bouncing as she waited.

"After school, I can share more of the story with you," I responded. "Okay? My locker?"

I tried not to sound sad, so she wouldn't be upset, but I knew it was best to wait.

When I met Sarah, I highlighted the weekend's woes without trying to vent all the sorry details. Sarah listened.

"You didn't walk all the way from the station," Sarah said.

"I did. I needed time to think about what had happened."

"Don't give up on your music, Molly. Just because you've had a setback …"

Sarah meant well as she tried to encourage me. At that moment, I was unable to accept her positivity, but I thanked her for trying.

"Sarah, I believe in God."

At first, she looked a little surprised at this interjection of a spiritual topic. Then, I asked, "Do you?"

"Yes. I do, Molly. What are you getting at, and how does that fit with what you feel?"

"I've been taught that God has good purposes for me, but everything keeps getting all messed up."

"Yes, I can see that."

"Sarah, I really need to know what God wants. Between now and graduation, I hope to figure it out. Obviously, none of my plans are working."

"I hope you find what you're looking for," Sarah said, giving me a gentle pat on the shoulder.

After school, I slipped into our apartment, hoping to remain unheard, and walked straight to my room.

"I'm home," I said, not waiting for Mama to answer. I clicked my door closed, and burrowed in my sanctuary.

Mama had placed some letters on my bed. I quickly glanced at the return addresses and noticed that Jack had written. I ripped the letter open with anticipation. I so wanted to hear his encouragement.

> Dear Molly,
>
> I really have missed our time together, even in the simple ways our lives crossed at school. I miss your notes in my locker too. I miss your sweet smile and your kind manner even more.
>
> Good news here. I am very excited to tell you that my parents are going to help me attend the symphony concert. My dad still has his job, and he agreed to help me pay for a ticket. I will repay mom and dad for the ticket, but they said they can wait until school is out. I don't know what the future holds since college is no longer possible. Maybe I can go later when the economy improves. Pray for me to know what to do about a finding work. Thanks.
>
> Anyway, in closing, Winnie's parents are going to go with us on the Interurban to Detroit. So, both Winnie and I will be there for your

victory concert. I can't wait.

Love,

Jack

In disbelief, I began weeping. Imagining all the happiness lost and unfulfilled dreams, I yielded to my grief again. Loss compounded. Where is your peace that passes all understanding, Lord? Help me. This is too hard.

When Mama called me for dinner, I pretended I was sound asleep. She knocked on the door. I had already turned off the light, and was camouflaged in my pile of covers.

"Molly? Don't you want any dinner, dear?"

"No, Mama. Not feeling well. You two go ahead."

Eventually, I cried myself to sleep that night. The next morning, I rallied my courage to read the other letter. It was from Winnie, but I didn't have the heart for more disappointment after reading Jack's news.

Dear Molly,

Your big day is almost here, and I can hardly wait to give you a hug. My parents and I are going to meet you at the train station and make certain you get to Orchestra Hall safely. Have you heard from Jack? He is trying to get the money together to come too. If I am this excited, I can barely imagine what you must be feeling. Your dream is coming true, Molly. Beautiful answered prayers.

On a more personal note, just so you know the latest, Wally and I are growing closer each passing week. I believe he is 'the one' for me. Forever. Since I won't be able to go on to college

> right now, Wally and I are talking about maybe getting married next summer. I know. Marriage sounds so limiting and mundane to a rising concert pianist. However, I'm only telling you now because I would love for you to be in my wedding, whenever it is. Of course, if Wally can't get work, all of this will be put on hold until he has a way to feed us. Whoever would have imagined I would be talking like this even a few months ago. I will see you soon, my dear friend.
>
> Much love and hugs,
>
> Winnie

Resisting the urge to indulge in one more self-pitying bawl, I washed my face, and dressed for school. I was encouraged by the love in Winnie's letter, but surprised by her talk of marriage. It almost made sense given our upside-down world.

My emotional venting the night before had exhausted me. Convincing Mama that I felt better, I ate a bowl of oatmeal, and gave her a goodbye hug, so I could distract myself for a few hours. At least I would have job skills in only a few months.

Though nothing could quite lift my spirits, the days did pass, one by one, without much active engagement on my part. I went to school. I did a little homework. I helped Mama with meals, and retreated to my room. Then, when a weekend came, I would sleep as late as Mama would let me. Then, I checked another week off my calendar. And another went by. I walked through my days like a marionette, waiting for my strings to be pulled this way and that. I was numb—functioning, but not feeling anything.

For the first time since I was little, I felt no purpose,

no direction. After graduation, I would figure out what life held beyond the confines of my parents. If God had something good for my life, he had not yet revealed it. I knew I must find new thinking in this new life.

One morning, I saw Sarah waving me down before we entered Mrs. Johnson's classroom.

"Molly, I had a grand idea come to me last night," Sarah said.

I forced a polite smile and waited in silence.

"You know how many people are out of work and doing poorly right now?" she began with enthusiasm belying her topic.

Not understanding her excitement over such a pathetic subject, I responded with sarcasm.

"No. Tell me how many."

"No, no. I didn't mean for you to tell me a number. I wanted you to think about how people are hurting these days," Sarah said.

"Okay. I have that image. What's your point?" I asked, slightly annoyed with her joy.

"What if we got permission to put on a concert? It would be free, and might cheer everybody up."

"That's nice," I said, still unmoved.

"Would you be willing to perform? Mr. Kahn, the orchestra teacher, said he would work with us. It could be a benefit concert—a benefit for everyone."

"I don't think so, Sarah. I am focused on finishing school and that's it right now."

I glanced at the floor, unwilling to make eye contact

while rejecting her idea.

"Would you please, please think about it, Molly?" Sarah pleaded. "It's not for you, or for me—it's for lots of people who need to be encouraged. Music lifts spirits."

"Okay, okay. I will think it over," I said, wanting to flee Sarah's pressure.

That evening before bedtime, I read my devotions and came upon Psalm 47. I read, "Take delight in the Lord, and he will give you your heart's desires."

I remembered Sarah's words: "It's not about you. It's not about me."

Maybe that was it. Had I been too self-absorbed? My gift of music. My career. My thrill of success. Me, me, me.

Oh, God, help me. I know the Bible says that you draw close to the brokenhearted. I am more than brokenhearted, Lord. I'm broken into tiny pieces. Take my plans, please, in exchange for yours, whatever they are. Show me your will, please.

Reflecting on my prayers as I lay there in the darkness, I confessed my selfishness again. I was a shattered and broken vessel. A quiet peace settled over me.

If I were ever to become whole again, I knew it would not be because of my own actions. What do you have in store, Lord? Do you still have a purpose for me?

Chapter 26—The Gift is Alive

God's message still resonated in my spirit as I rose the next morning. "It's not about me." Okay. I would give it my best shot. I didn't know what that was, but I had nothing to lose. After all, I had no direction and graduation was still a few months away. No concertizing for this kiddo. No Jack. No Winnie.

When I saw Sarah in English, I passed her a note.

"You don't have to answer," I whispered.

My communication was simple: "God used you."

Sarah unfolded the note discreetly before Mrs. Johnson began calling the roll. I watched her expression change to a beautiful smile. With a nod and a wink of her eye, I knew we had a deal.

"Good morning, students," Mrs. Johnson began. "In the next few weeks, we're going to review diagraming."

I glanced around the room, stifling my instinct to laugh. The students' expressions were priceless as they considered her exciting news in disbelief.

To bolster support, she went on. "You must realize, students, that diagramming will improve your writing skills by and by."

After demonstrating the fine art of labeling sentence components once again, Mrs. Johnson assigned us practice exercises—many practice exercises. When the bell finally rang, we sprang out of our seats, ready to flee the agony of our joyless task. Sarah waited for me.

"My, my, but that was tedious, wasn't it, Molly?" We both laughed after we were out of Mrs. Johnson's hearing.

"The whole time I was diagramming, I kept thinking about your note, Molly. I can't figure out what God has to do with my question about the concert," she said.

"I'll explain later, but for now, just know that I will perform. I'll do everything I can to help with your idea."

"I can't wait to hear how God changed your mind. I will talk to Mr. Kahn this afternoon during orchestra, unless you want to come too."

"Ask if he thinks we can have the concert first. Then we can work together on the organizing, if you'd like."

"Great, Molly. Thank you," she replied, grinning.

Mr. Kahn agreed on the spot. Soon, students and faculty alike were buzzing with the idea of giving back to the Lincoln Park neighborhood in this way. When I talked to Pastor Thomas, he volunteered the church building for our big night, Saturday, April 19, 1930.

Announcement fliers were made in business classes, and students delivered them to the area stores. "Let Music Brighten Your Life" they read. The idea grew within our school and became something positive. Everyone rallied around the project. Auditions were necessary because so many people wanted to take part—solo voices, quartets, the glee club, instrumentalists, and our small, albeit pitiful-sounding, orchestra. We even had some students who worked up a short comedy skit.

Those who didn't want to perform were eager to help promote the idea. Some students went door to door inviting families who might not have contacts at Waller. Students volunteered to usher. The project brought a contagious excitement to Waller High School.

April blessed Chicago with sunshine, spring showers, and the promise of summer not too far away. Saturday, April 19, arrived without rain to mar our celebration, but the show would have gone on regardless. Waller High School families and friends started streaming in by six-thirty. You could hear the buzzing voices, and friends greeting friends.

Mama introduced herself as we stood in a lengthy line. "We are the Martin family, new to the area, recently having moved to Chicago from Royal Oak," she said often.

"Oh, it is nice to meet you. We moved down from Detroit after Black Friday took my husband's job," a middle-aged woman said in response. "My name is Mary," the lady said, "and my daughter, Mildred, is playing the flute tonight." Mama smiled while the men stood behind and shook hands. I didn't know Mildred, but we had met during rehearsal.

By seven o'clock, the sanctuary was overflowing with people. Mr. Benson, the head Principal of Waller, went to the front of the sanctuary as our Master of Ceremony.

"I want to welcome everyone to this special Saturday night out. Those of you just entering, come on in. Stand or sit wherever you can."

"We are thankful for some student leaders who thought this would be a good idea. Thank you, Sarah, Molly, and Mr. Kahn, our orchestra director, who made this event possible. Let the fun begin!"

A quartet of students opened the evening with, "Happy Days Are Here Again," and "Singin' in the Rain." They sounded so good, it made everyone feel like tapping their toes to their lighthearted tunes.

One of the teachers, Mr. Baker from the math department, imitated Al Jolson singing "All the Clouds'll Roll Away." Who knew he could sing? The students applauded vigorously. As I looked into the crowd, I saw row upon row of relaxed, smiling faces.

"Thank you, Lord," I whispered, glancing over at Father and Mama beside me, smiling at the happy tunes. It appeared that Sarah's brainstorm was working. Everyone seemed relieved to have a break from their troubles. The orchestra played a few show tunes, off-tune, but with zippy enthusiasm. Mr. Benson belted out "Keep Your Sunny Side Up!" with instruments for backup: "Keep your funny side up, up. Let your laughter ring through, through. Stand upon your legs. Be like two fried eggs. Keep your sunny side up!" The people laughed at the funny lyrics, and clapped heartily when he finished.

More serious music was mixed into the fun like Mr. Thompson and his classical cello piece. I accompanied a flute solo Sarah played so beautifully. Mr. Kahn had asked me to end the program that night. I knew the concerto could not be played by our beginning orchestra. I also knew that its melancholy melody represented my lost aspirations, and that was not what this was about. A performance of the Rachmaninoff Concerto was for another time, and another place, if ever again.

The Baldwin Acrosonic piano had been rolled into the sanctuary for our concert—but not up on the platform. It would be in the way of other contributing performers. It was placed in the center on the floor level. When the evening was about to conclude, I knew it was my time. I stepped forward to once again be seated before an audience. I recalled the thrill of my lifetime when I played with the symphony. With hands poised above the keys, in that always stirring moment before playing, I felt a deep peace rising within me. Uncharacteristically, I lifted my eyes. They met the image of Christ in a beautiful composition of stained-glass. He had been there all along, but I hadn't encountered him.

Looking up at the altar, I knew why I was there in that distinct time and place. Tears began to trickle slowly from the corners of my eyes. How could I have been so blind? From the bottom of my heart, I keenly understood what God was working into my life. This performance was not about me, as he had so clearly shown me. Just as Sarah had said.

Here I sit, Lord, in front of your altar. I choose to yield my gift, Lord, for your use—to glorify you. Not me.

I began Beethoven's Sonata no. 8, the famous "Pathétique," a part of the repertoire I'd studied over the past year. Its intensity emulated Rachmaninoff's Concerto in C minor, without the symphonic accompaniment. Though the church piano was not in perfect tune, the spirit of God's love could not be quenched.

I was overwhelmed with joy that evening, the peace that we cannot create on our own. This time, I knew I was playing for his pleasure. His presence reassured me, even as I played. The gift of music was yet alive in me, if only … if only, I placed it in his hands. At last, I understood. In the yielding of his gift to bless others, he would also bless me.

I rose to a standing ovation, exhilarated, yet acutely aware of the change in my heart. Personal acclaim was not what this was about. It was his gift, and it had always been his gift. I was grateful I was his chosen vessel. I bowed in thanks to the appreciative audience.

Then, I turned to the image of Christ at the altar behind me, and extended my arms in thanksgiving to the one who had shared his life and love. I had found his peace, at last, the peace which passes all human understanding. Thank you, Lord, for showing me that your ways are higher than mine.

> The Lord is my strength and my shield; my heart trusted in him, and I am helped: therefore my heart greatly rejoiceth; and with my song will I praise him. (Psalm 28:7 KJV)

Epilogue

August 1930

I rose early, as usual these days, and took my Bible to the sofa in the living room. Opening to Philippians 4, I read my meditation for that day, that memorable day—my first day to return to Royal Oak since our move. "Be careful for nothing; but in every thing by prayer and supplication with thanksgiving let your requests be made known unto God."

Thank you, Lord, for getting me this far. Thank you for taking my worries. Thank you for everything you have brought me through—my losses and my victories.

My eyes dropped to the next verse. "And the peace of God, which passeth all understanding, shall keep your hearts and minds through Christ Jesus.

I will trust you for your answers to my future, Lord, and I praise you for my peace.

Feeling encouraged, I then called to Father. "I'm ready, and it's time to leave."

Father drove me to the train station. Yes, he drove me to this same beautiful station where I hopelessly left my dream of getting back to Detroit. There were no threatening blizzards on this hot summer day. No, indeed. I had purchased my own ticket, paid for with my small earnings from working at the Marshall Fields Department Store. It was not a dream job, but it was a paying job. My manager had suggested that maybe in another year I might be able to work as one of their in-store models. I decided "tall and thin" wasn't too bad after all. That's what Mrs. Jackson said she needed in her models.

Today was a milestone, for sure. As the train chugged along to my familiar and beloved hometown, I could hardly believe all that had happened since December. Winnie was getting married to Wally, and I was going to be in their wedding that day. It was hard to imagine my best friend married, but in only a few hours, she would be forever yoked to her sweetheart. Such a smart cookie she was, but not many people were going to college these days to gain educational opportunities. Who could afford it? Wally was going to work for his father at the gas station until better opportunities came along. I knew they would be fine together, one way or another.

So much had happened the summer after high school. Father had been right. With the beach only a few blocks away, I made some new friends. Jack and I still corresponded, but I also got to know some other boys that summer. A handsome young blond named Joey made it clear he was sweet on me. He was a few years older than I was, and in the plus column, Joey had a steady income. He seemed eager to find a special someone and settle down. Me? Not so much.

The train slowed to a creep as it pulled into Royal Oak. My excitement swelled with every chug-a-chug and slowing lurch. Jack would be my ride since I would arrive a short time before the wedding. Winnie's family would be too busy, for sure.

Stepping off the train, I spotted my Jack, waiting with open arms. He waved big, and approached the platform with his bright smile flashing.

"Oh, Molly, what a beautiful sight you are."

He lifted me off the ground, and swung me around with my feet flying. We were both laughing like the old days.

"It is so good to have you here, Molly. Do you need to eat, or are you fine until after the wedding?"

"I'll wait, Jack. I'm so excited, I probably couldn't eat right now anyway."

"Here's our chariot-of-choice for the day," Jack announced, pointing at an old blue Ford Model T his dad had loaned him.

"Great," I said, overjoyed to have any kind of personal transportation.

I smiled as I watched Jack driving. About that time Jack glanced over, beaming from ear to ear.

What a sweet soul he was. He had been such a faithful friend through all my dramas. Did he still care for me deeply, this wonderful guy, my first love, Jack?

We drove directly to the church, so I wouldn't be late for any last-minute preparations. Only a few friends and family were invited, with a simple reception to follow at Winnie's house. Walking into the church, I immediately spied a dear old friend. I couldn't believe Winnie had forgotten to tell me Mr. Clancy was playing for her wedding. Perhaps, he needed some extra money, or maybe he was doing this as a favor for the family. I didn't know, but I had to go give him a quick hug before the wedding began.

"Mr. Clancy!" I cried, my pace quickening into a lady-like dash to the front. "Look at you—here to help us celebrate my best friend's wedding vows."

He stood up in surprise.

"Why, Molly, I'm so happy to see you," he announced with a big smile.

"I had to come say how happy I am to see you. Are you

doing well? And Mrs. Clancy?"

He paused. "Mrs. Clancy passed late last spring, Molly."

"I am sad to hear," I said, waiting to see if he wanted to talk more.

"It's been hard, but I'm now eighty-five. I know I will see my Martha before too long."

"I'm sure you must miss her. Are you still teaching?"

"Only a little here and there," he answered. "Hard times, you know."

"I do know, Mr. Clancy," I said with empathy. "Here now. You should sit down to rest."

I heard Jack call me from the back of the sanctuary.

"Molly, Winnie wants you."

"Coming now," I said. Looking into Mr. Clancy's tired, weathered face, I said, "Mr. Clancy, you'll never know how you encouraged me."

"Whatever do you mean? In music?"

"Yes, in music, but more. You said God had a good plan for my life, and I should trust him. I held onto that Scripture when my dreams went up in smoke."

I leaned over to give him a gentle kiss on the cheek.

"Thank you so much for everything, Mr. Clancy."

I waved a goodbye, and hurried back to find Winnie.

"She's in the room on the left," Jack said.

I poked my head into the dressing room. There stood my dearest friend in a simple white dress her mother had once worn at her own wedding. She looked radiant, and beautiful, as always.

"Winnie," I said, trying to stifle my tears of happiness.

Such a soulmate she was, and oh, how I had missed being a part of her daily life for all those months. We hugged, and tried not to cry to spare our makeup. In what seemed like only a few minutes, it was time to begin the ceremony.

There wouldn't be a grand processional with the Mendelssohn "Wedding March," but I was sure Mr. Clancy would play something joyful for the occasion. Jack was Wally's best man, and I was Winnie's maid of honor. How ironic. Here we were, standing together for this beautiful marriage ceremony. It seemed only days ago when we were meeting at our lockers.

I heard the words of the pastor, "… for better or worse, in sickness and in health ..."

My mind was whirling as I looked over at Jack, my sweet prince of a guy. Would Jack be in my future? I could not even imagine how my story would unfold. He caught my glance, and winked back. Priceless.

"You may kiss your bride," the pastor pronounced.

Wally kissed Winnie tenderly as we all witnessed their commitment to marriage for a lifetime. Mr. Clancy began a rousing recessional as Jack escorted me out of the church following the bride and groom.

Lord, I cannot see my future, but I know you do. So, once again, I place the rest of my days into your care. You are the only one who can bring joy out of mourning and peace in the darkness. It is you I trust. It is only you who can give me peace. Amen. Thank you, Lord, for this beautiful day.

Afterword

The legacy of the main character in this novel is a testimony to her many prayers. The story is based on a true character, Mildred M. Isle, known as Molly in the book. Despite Mildred's unfulfilled dream in real life, her son was profoundly inspired by her passion for music. Mildred was blessed to be able to see her son, Robert J. Isle, work hard, develop his talent, and earn recognition in the world of professional music.

Robert gained recognition playing his trumpet while still in high school, just as his mother had in piano performance. His honors were many, as he earned a full scholarship at the University of Kansas, toured as a member of the American Wind Symphony, held a position with the Kansas City Philharmonic, and played musicals as first trumpet at Kansas City Starlight Theater. He was a member of The United States Marine Band in Washington, DC, participating in four nationwide tours, and performing at the White House many times.

Robert earned a Master's Degree in Music from The Catholic University of America, studying with Lloyd Geisler, Principal Trumpet and Associate Conductor with the National Symphony. He played lead trumpet at the Kennedy Center for eight years, and performed numerous musicals at Shady Grove, Wolf Trap Theater, and Arena Stage, all in the Washington, DC, area.

My brother's profession was greatly influenced by our

mother's talent and positive "You Can Do It" philosophy. Our mother was also practical, having lived through the Great Depression, and insisted my brother earn an education degree, so he could teach as well as perform. Robert was able to make his dreams come true, completing this circle of family history, and Mildred's legacy was fulfilled in the next generation. I give God the praise and glory for answering our mother's prayers and giving me the opportunity to tell the story.

About the Author

Joan's passion for people, writing, and teaching has been with her since childhood. A transplanted Midwesterner who has claimed Virginia as her home since the 1980s, she earned a BS in elementary education and a MSE with an emphasis on reading instruction from the University of Kansas. While teaching middle schoolers the joy of reading young adult fiction, she observed a dearth of stories embedded with wholesome virtues and ideals, and decided to do something about it.

Drawing on her years of experience as a reading specialist, Joan began developing ancillary reading materials (fiction, nonfiction, and poetry) for reading programs, supplemental leveled reading books, and teaching guides, for numerous educational publishers. As her love for sharing God's truth matured, her ambitions turned to writing young adult novels embedded with inspirational and biblical concepts.

Joan grew up in a musical family, learned to play the piano as a young child, and performed often as a teenager. Though Joan did not major in music at the university, her mother was a recognized classical pianist and teacher, and her brother made a career of performance in trumpet. Joan has sung in church choirs and participated in worship ministries for many years. She has engaged in children's ministry roles such as teaching Sunday School and leading children's choirs. She has led children's Christian clubs in her home, in churches, and as a teacher/sponsor of an after-school club at the middle-school level. She has served at local crisis pregnancy centers for over twenty years as a receptionist, a board member, and most recently, as a counselor/patient advocate.

Joan is the proud mother of two adult children—a son, Shannon Burnett, and a daughter, Kristi West. She has also had the privilege of being a stepmom to two adult daughters, Michele Huck, and Pamela Quinn. She considers herself a bragging-rights grandmother of eight cherished grandchildren.